THE GLASS FORTRESS

BY
M.C. BECHUM

PublishAmerica
Baltimore

Softcover 9781451279283
PUBLISHED BY PUBLISHAMERICA, LLLP
www.publishamerica.com
Baltimore

Printed in the United States of America

THE GLASS FORTRESS

My name is Pete Masters. As a private investigator in the Panhandle city of Burnadett, Florida, I'm fairly accustomed to a variety of natural disasters. I've seen telephone poles snapped in half by tornadoes and the landscape of a Northwest Florida county draped in a blanket of snow. I've lived through three-digit temperatures in the month of June and walked around in a windbreaker near the end of August. Without a doubt, Florida's weather can be dangerous as well as unpredictable. Yet, the most heartrending destruction has commonly been set in motion by human hands. The fires that plagued parts of the Tri-state area a few years ago were no exception.

The temperature was unusually warm for the beginning of spring. The Governor had issued a statewide burn ban due to extremely dry conditions. Additional blazes were being reported throughout parts of Alabama and Southern Georgia. Yet, despite the need for extra precautions and concern for their neighbors, residents continued about their daily routines. Yes, for those who made a living and raised families, life had to go on. Unfortunately, that meant even longer hours for the already overworked first responders.

Aside from the everyday grind of maintaining law and order, a segment of the Burnadett P.D. had been selected to be a part of the Internet Predator Task Force headed by my friend, Sergeant Roy Van Eason.

I'd known Roy since high school and though no one asked for my recommendation, I would've been the first to sing the praises of this blond, blue-eyed, southern gentleman. For the past fifteen years, he'd worn that navy blue uniform and performed his duty with the utmost of integrity. Although the sternly built flatfoot wanted to protect children from abusers, he thoroughly opposed the alliance the Police Commissioner had formed with WKGC-TV 16.

The station's most popular newsman, Miles Trenton, hosted a weekly telecast that exposed internet predators on camera before police moved in to make the arrest.

Any viewer with access to network television had to know Trenton's hard-hitting productions weren't the result of local media brainstorming. Nevertheless, it had elevated a mediocre reporter to the status of regional celebrity.

The intrusion of the press wasn't the only concern on the mind of Sergeant Van Eason. He also dreaded the fallout that could result if one of his cops made a mistake on film. While the veteran crime fighter was committed to protecting the innocent, he had no desire to advance his career by besmirching the records of his fellow officers. Consequently, it was that kind of devotion that compelled his superiors to place him at the helm of the most scrutinized operation the city had seen in decades.

Van Eason was stationed at an empty residence on Boliva Road. The stings took place in the two-story brick house across the street where Trenton and his camera crew waited with the Department's young-looking decoy. So far, a throng of sexual predators had been captured and convicted after taking the bait that led to this house. The system seemed fool-proof. That was until the humid spring morning a desperate father named Michael Stewart entered the driveway and stepped out of his car.

The house used to belong to a repeated sex offender named Clark Milford. After his last arrest, authorities confiscated his computer and other materials connected to his crimes. From the journals and photographs found in the home, Van Eason's detectives ascertained that the suspect had been corresponding with someone who used the name "Little-Girl-Lost."

That was also the screen name used by Michael Stewart's daughter, Connie.

Connie was a sixteen year old rebel whose life had spiraled out-of-control. Though her embattled father had done everything in his power to shield the girl from the snares of a culture poised to draw her in and destroy her, his warnings fell upon deaf ears. Finally, the calamities he'd imagined became the teen's reality.

Connie was believed to have been abducted by an internet predator. Her tormented dad had spent countless nights roaming the streets and showing his child's picture to indifferent strangers. Sadly, after two months of manhunts and amber alerts, the trail had gone cold. To the dismay of the family, investigators were beginning to fear the worst.

Ironically, Sergeant Van Eason had been telling me about the eerie email that was sent to Clark Milford a few hours before I arrived. Little-Girl-Lost corresponded with the suspect by way of instant message. Throughout the course of their conversation, Milford made himself out to be a pubescent disaster yearning for someone to understand him. Maintaining the same front wasn't easy for the Sergeant's team, but with the help of previous emails and a few entries discovered in Milford's diary, they'd managed to construct a believable portrait of the individual who called himself "Shattered Dreamer." Though there was no way to prove Milford had been in physical contact with Connie, the information he had made police confident that she was the teenager on the other end of the line. Moreover, even if they turned out to be wrong, at the very least, another runaway would be off the street.

CHAPTER 2

I was watching Milford's former residence on the three monitors that had been set up in the house across the street when I heard Sergeant Van Eason open the front door. Despite the humid conditions outside, the place was a little drafty and the floor could have used a good waxing. However, there was running water and the dingy green walls did give the room that lived-in feel.

"Anything happen while I was gone, Pete?" he asked, as he entered the room with a carry out bag from the local coffee house.

"Not yet," I replied. "What makes you think this Milford character could be the key to finding Connie Stewart?"

"Milford had information that sounded very convincing," he said, handing me a styrofoam cup before slipping out of his windbreaker and taking a seat.

"Like what?" I asked, sitting down beside him.

"He mentioned meeting the girl at the Bop-and-Go convenience store in Vernon. Apparently, she and a tall boyfriend with a ponytail were driving a Corvette. When the boyfriend ran down the street, Milford, who was washing windows at the time, walked over to converse with her. I doubt she was aware of his unwholesome intentions."

"I wouldn't think so."

"But there's something else that bothers me."

"What's that?"

"If the man she was with felt comfortable enough to leave Connie alone with the car, there's no reason to believe she was there against her will."

"Can you get Milford to clarify what he saw that day?"

"Are you kidding? That clown's lips are sealed tighter than the Pentagon. His lawyer has advised him to clam up until the trial."

I took a sip of coffee and caught sight of something moving on the screen. An aqua blue four-door sedan was approaching Milford's house. Roy picked up his radio just as the dispatch from one of his men came in.

"Station-one to Base," the officer said. "It looks like we've got a live one coming to you, Sarge."

"Everybody just sit tight," the Sergeant instructed. "Let the news people do their thing first. They'll give us the signal."

We didn't immediately recognize the driver. Two months of sleepless nights and a five o'clock shadow had altered the countenance of Michael Stewart. Though we hadn't been formally introduced, I'd taken an interest in his daughter's case and reviewed Police files concerning her disappearance. While I hadn't learned anything new, I remained willing to provide any assistance needed. I'd also listened to witness testimony and interviews that gave me a little insight into the people involved. The picture I'd composed of this worried father was complex and disheartening.

It appeared that the imposing citadel of accepted beliefs and unquestioned platitudes that sheltered his world was in serious danger of crumbling down around him. The ingratiating beacon that once illuminated the path of this forty-six year old insurance agent had grown dim and misleading. In the aftermath of life's torrential squalls, heartrending traumas and personal loss left the man who thought he had everything wondering if rainbows really do exist.

In the past five years, Michael had mourned the death of his first wife and watched helplessly as his daughter became someone he didn't know. He couldn't bear the thought of someone abusing his baby girl. Finding her was now the most important thing in this distraught family man's life and he was prepared to use all the resources at his disposal to bring the teenager home.

For a principled conformist who'd grown up with the deep-rooted values of the early sixties, the misfortune that had invaded Michael's sanctum made him feel betrayed. From the moment he learned to walk, the civic-minded altruist's existence had been anchored in the conviction that he would be rewarded for every selfless deed. Safely guarded within the walls of a seemingly impenetrable stronghold, this classic American postulator naively pursued his dreams with every confidence he'd overcome defeat by maintaining a positive attitude and the purest of motives. Regrettably, when the violent winds of adversity laid siege upon the very structure of a life he was sure he understood, the petrified castaway was ill-prepared to ride out the storm.

Michael had come to know about the house on Boliva Road because Connie's best friend, Karen, had just returned home from visiting her grandparents. After receiving word the girl she loved like a sister might have been abducted by a predator, Karen brought Michael the laptop Connie kept hidden. An agonizing sifting of possible passwords eventually afforded the savvy parent access to his daughter's emails. He then initiated a dialogue with the person he believed to be Shattered Dreamer. So when he was invited to visit the house at 3594 Boliva Road, Michael prepared to confront this mysterious stranger. Curiously, presuming the cop on the other end of the line was his daughter's abductor wasn't the gravest mistake he could've made.

Michael was packing a .38 caliber revolver. He'd purchased the weapon two years earlier when a gang of thugs began terrorizing the neighborhood. The law-abiding working stiff had never even fired the piece. For a quiet man who'd always strived to turn the other cheek, the prospect of having to take a human life seared his conscience like a branding iron. Even in the formal setting of a Police interview room he'd wondered aloud what he could've done to deserve the anguish that had overtaken him. His world was spinning out of control. It was the darkest time he'd ever endured. Sadly, the worst was yet to come.

CHAPTER 3

Although an army of police officers were stationed all around him, Michael didn't appear to detect their presence as he parked his car in the driveway. Even in his precarious state of mind, I could understand why he would've been oblivious to a setup. The manicured lawn and flourishing flowers made the place look like something out of a magazine. On the other hand, the gloomy overcast sky didn't do a lot to improve the ambiance.

Sergeant Van Eason and I quietly monitored the anxious prober's every move.

"That fellow looks familiar," Roy said.

"I hope he's not a member of the Department," I responded.

Though his motives were unknown to us at the time, Michael's actions were actually quite daring. After all, he had no way of knowing what awaited him on the other side of that door. For all he knew, Shattered Dreamer was a seasoned masher who'd learned to spot the slightest hint of danger. Entering this house might have brought an ordinary dad face to face with one of the most vicious animals on two legs. Ironically, the vermin planning to devour Michael's flesh had never even been arrested.

The saga of Miles Trenton could best be conveyed as a romantic fairytale that gradually eroded into a mindless tragedy. The boyish good looks that once opened doors for this over-the-hill reporter were now the products of skillful lighting and a makeup artist who didn't miss a trick. His flawless smile and enamoring green eyes were no longer capable of concealing the vainglorious monster with the insatiable appetite for self-fulfillment. The callous playboy loved the spotlight and he was willing to do whatever it took to maintain his place at the top. For an unscrupulous manipulator like Trenton, that meant taking advantage of every opportunity.

Though the past few years hadn't been particularly kind to the salt-and-pepper haired correspondent with the vast collection of double-breasted suits, he'd managed to capitalize on his role as the city's best known child protector. In fact, the Internet Predator segment's success had afforded the cunning news hawk the respect and appreciation of the entire community. Most people viewed him as a crusader for the innocent who wouldn't rest until every abuser was behind bars. However, there was a side of Miles Trenton that was seldom seen by the general public.

When faced with the possibility of losing all he'd lied and swindled to attain, this audacious hoodlum was capable of unleashing a hurricane of brutality that could bring the most intrepid opposer to his knees. He'd done favors for more than a few crime bosses around town and he wasn't afraid to call in a marker from time to time. When a man made the mistake of crossing Trenton, he could expect a crash course in criminal behavior facilitated by a scholarship to the school of hard knocks. Unfortunately, Michael Stewart would be receiving his degree with honors.

When Michael stepped out of his car and approached the recently renovated brick home with the sandalwood shutters, the nervous amateur investigator's entrance looked like a replay from a very familiar scene. His first rap on the door garnered an immediate response.

"Come in," uttered an angelic voice from inside the house. "It's not locked."

Michael walked in and looked around the sparsely furnished room. The sofa and recliner a few steps to his right were brand new. That plush lime-green carpet appeared to have been freshly shampooed. The laminated floor in the L-shaped kitchen reeked of wax. The smell of pine cleaner also lingered in the air. The perplexed caller looked terrified. He was about to fly the coop when a young women emerged from the bedroom in slippers and a robe.

"Did you have any trouble finding the place?" she asked.

"There must be some mistake," Michael muttered. "I was supposed to meet a man here."

"Oh don't worry," she told him. "My parents are going to be out of town until the end of the week. Just make yourself comfortable while I go back and finish my shower."

"I don't know what's going on!" Michael stammered, heading for the door. "I've got to get out of here."

Michael had almost made it out when Miles Trenton parted the black curtains on the far side of the room and made his presence known.

"What is this?" the cornered prey demanded, as he recognized the famous newsman. "You're Miles Trenton."

That's right," he confirmed with a self-assured smirk. "Since you know who I am, I presume you know we're on television."

"Television? What's happening here?"

"We're investigating adults who have inappropriate relationships with minors. That young woman you just spoke with is an undercover police officer."

"You don't understand!" the frantic dupe contended. "I'm not interested in having any relationships with minors. My name is Michael Stewart. My daughter has been missing for the past two months. I came to this address to meet a slimy piece of garbage who calls himself Shattered Dreamer."

Van Eason dropped his coffee and sprang to his feet! "I knew that guy looked familiar," he said. "I've got to get him out of there!"

"This is crazy," I commented.

The Sergeant picked up the radio receiver. "Base Commander to all units," he said. "I'm going to approach the house. Everyone hold your positions. I repeat; stay put."

"Want me to go with you, Roy?" I asked.

"No, I want you to stay here and monitor the situation. A reunion between you and Trenton is the last thing anybody needs."

Though my first inclination was to back Roy up, I had to admit his perception was right on the money. Miles Trenton and I were not on the best of terms and an altercation would only make matters worse. That ambitious thug was dangerous. To our dismay, we hadn't seen anything yet.

CHAPTER 4

Michael Stewart's pleas for understanding meant nothing to Miles Trenton. The malicious destroyer had zoned in on his target and was prepared to fire.

"Are you a friend of Shattered Dreamer?" the delving reporter asked Michael.

"I've never met the man," the bewildered father assured him. "I only know he spoke to my daughter a few weeks ago and I wanted to see what he could tell me."

"I've got to be honest with you, Michael. We've heard a lot of strange stories since we began this series, but yours really takes the cake."

"Are you insane? A teenage girl's life is at stake and all you can think about is making me your next big scoop. You haven't changed a bit."

"What?"

"I suppose a weasel like you would have forgotten by now. So let me refresh your memory. Several years ago, Sarah and Norman Baterman were accused of taking part in terrorist attacks against various political leaders around the country. There was no concrete evidence against them, but that didn't stop you. You hounded them day and night. Their reputations were destroyed. They lost their jobs. Even their children had to move away to find work. You made their lives miserable."

"That wasn't too long after 9-11," Trenton insisted. The safety of this entire community demanded that I make every effort to learn the truth. If I'd been remiss, a threat to national security might have gone unnoticed."

"You didn't work so hard to protect the Baterman's security once the FBI determined that the only connection they had to the real terrorists was an antique rifle Norman sold fifteen years ago."

"The station ran a story admitting our mistake."

"You aired a thirty minute spot that ran one night."

"I lived up to my responsibilities," Trenton responded.

"Try explaining that to the grandchildren who won't be spending anymore summers with the Baterman's," Michael insisted.

"What do you mean?"

"A few days after your little apology graced the airways, someone abducted Norman and Sarah. Their bodies were discovered at the bottom of the Chipola River. So don't tell me about your responsibilities, Mr. Trenton. You are and always will be a self-centered opportunist who'll do anything to get your story. Well I hope you're enjoying the prominence you've extracted from the blood of your victims. A couple of very decent people had to pay a heavy price for your success."

Trenton couldn't believe the audacity of this man. The boiling correspondent's face turned red as he crinkled the roll of papers in his hand. He wasn't about to let some suspected pedophile embarrass him in front of his crew.

Without warning, Trenton grabbed Michael by the lapels of his coat and forced the indignant father's back into the wall! The livid crime boss drew back to strike his victim, but before he could claim his vengeance, Sergeant Van Eason came charging through the front door!

"Stop the taping!" Van Eason demanded, as he looked to his left and observed what the malicious news anchor was about to do. "What's going on in here?"

"It was just a misunderstanding," Trenton explained, unhanding Michael.

"Is that right, Mr. Stewart?" the Sergeant asked.

Trenton was surprised to hear the officer address his suspect by name. "You know him?" he inquired.

"Of course," Van Eason confirmed. "This is Michael Stewart. His daughter has been missing for several weeks."

"I didn't realize," the daunted egomaniac muttered, straightening his tie. He signaled to his crew. "Shut it down, people."

"Why are you here, Mr. Stewart?" the Sergeant asked.

"Because a friend of Connie's found a laptop she'd kept hidden from me," he explained.

"I looked at the emails and discovered a lot of exchanges with someone who calls himself Shattered Dreamer. That's when I pretended to be my daughter online. I wanted to see what he could tell me."

"You should have called me," Van Eason told him. "Shattered Dreamer's real name is Clark Milford. We arrested him and confiscated his computer. There were a lot of emails from other predators. With the help of the decoy you've already met, we were able to lure a lot of them to this house."

"Then you saw the correspondence I sent him," Michael concluded.

"Yes I did," the Sergeant confirmed. "I didn't know what to anticipate when the person using the name Little-Girl-Lost got here. I certainly didn't expect to see you come walking up the driveway."

"I always suspected Connie was hiding something from me," Michael said, placing his hands on his hips. "I turned my house upside down. When Karen showed up with that computer, I thought I'd struck gold."

"I think I'd better take another look around your house this afternoon," Van Eason decided. "We might have missed something the last time."

Trenton noticed a bulge under Michael's coat. "Do you have a gun, Mr. Stewart?" he asked.

Reluctant to answer, the bombarded soldier of misfortune attempted to explain. "Well I thought there might be trouble," he said. "So I decided to bring some protection."

"Do you have a permit for the weapon?" Trenton probed further.

"I wasn't planning to shoot anyone," Michael told him.

"Alright, that's enough," Van Eason insisted.

"Are you kidding me?" Trenton responded. "This man is in possession of an illegal firearm. He should be arrested."

Finally, the moment Van Eason had been dreading was at hand. With the flip of a switch, this shiftless gossip monger could distort the motives of every politician and bureaucrat in town. The tormented Task Force Commander abhorred the thought of arresting a father who'd already suffered more than his share of heartache. Nevertheless, the eyes of the community were fixed firmly upon the Sergeant's every move and he couldn't afford the appearance of favoritism.

"Mr. Stewart, if you can't produce a permit, you'll have to come with me," Van Eason said, reaching for the perpetrator's revolver.

I watched Trenton carefully as Roy escorted Michael out. The veteran newshound looked very pleased. Though having the man who'd displayed such wanton disrespect taken away by the authorities should have satisfied the twisted narcissist's vengeful craving, I was certain he didn't feel the penalty was severe enough. Besides, the compassion Van Eason felt for Michael was obvious. Trenton had to believe the cop would go out of his way to protect the despondent father. A bull dog like Trenton had to see to it that Michael's ordeal sent a message to every tough guy with a death wish.

"That's a rap, crew!" the conniving wretch shouted, heading for the bathroom with his cell phone in hand.

I couldn't see what was going on when Trenton closed the door behind him, but I was convinced he was about to dial the number of an acquaintance who knew how to make bad things happen to good people. At any rate, the wheels of retribution were in motion and the designated path was certain. By journey's end, Trenton intended to trample the life and reputation of the man who'd defied him. It was a trip the malicious hoodlum had taken many times. Yet, when a man becomes accustomed to traveling in the dark, he can easily forget to pay attention to the things he cannot see.

CHAPTER 5

For most people, the thought of sitting alone in a cold drab interrogation room wouldn't evoke images of better days to come. However, Michael Stewart felt confident that his troubles with the law were about to be resolved. After five hours of mulling over every mistake he'd made in the past decade, he fully expected Sergeant Van Eason to come in and inform him that the State Attorney had decided to drop the charges. Any reasonable person with a modicum of empathy had to see that this hard-working family man was only trying to rescue his child. Sadly, the exhausted idealist was in for a rude awakening.

While Sergeant Van Eason was downstairs consulting with the Night watch Captain, I entered the interrogation room and sat down at the table across from Michael.

"Mr. Stewart, I'm Pete Masters," I told him. "I'm a private investigator."

"How much trouble am I in, Masters?" he asked.

"I'm not sure. Showing up with that gun was a bad move."

"Now you tell me."

"You've gone through a lot in the past few months. I doubt the people who run things want to look like their beating up on a suffering father."

"I want to believe that, but nothing has been keeping with tradition lately."

I took a breath and leaned forward. "It may not be easy to see right now, but the Sergeant has been doing everything in his power to bring your child home," I said. "He really is on your side."

If my words of encouragement did anything to make Michael feel better, the victory was short-lived. Because when the Sergeant did arrive, he wasn't exactly blown in by a whirlwind of faith.

The expression on Roy's face was perplexing as he entered the room with a file in his hand. "Is there anything you'd like to tell me, Mr. Stewart?" he asked.

"I don't know what you mean?" Michael responded.

Roy tossed the file down on the table in front of him. "Take a look," he said.

A frown of disgust swept over the detained father's face as he read a letter addressed to his daughter. "This is revolting!" he exclaimed. "Who would write something like this?"

"Are you saying this is the first time you've seen this letter?" Roy inquired.

"Of course," the repulsed parent confirmed. "Why would you even ask?"

"Because it was found in your daughter's room," Van Eason said.

"This is outrageous!" Michael exclaimed, pounding the table with his fist. "I'd never write a letter like that to Connie. I definitely wouldn't use this kind of language in her presence."

"I'm inclined to believe you, but there's another problem," Roy said.

"What could be worse than this?" I asked.

"The discovery of this letter sparks questions that can't be ignored," the Sergeant explained. "The State Attorney is very reluctant to go easy on a suspect who could be having an inappropriate relationship with his daughter."

"But I didn't write that letter!" Michael insisted.

Van Eason sat down and looked Michael in the eye. "I don't want you to go down on a weapons charge," he said. "I certainly don't want you branded as a child molester. But the press is breathing down my neck and the brass can't afford to look bad."

"The press?" Michael wondered aloud. "Trenton! He heard you say you wanted to search Connie's room again. That jerk planted the letter."

"That's right," I agreed, snapping my fingers. "When you took Mr. Stewart out, I saw Trenton take his cell phone into the bathroom."

"But you couldn't hear what he was saying in the bathroom," the Sergeant argued. "Without eye-witness testimony, Trenton's million-dollar lawyers will bury us."

"So what happens now?" Michael asked.

"I'll have to place you under arrest," Roy said, rising to his feet. "You've been advised of your rights. I'd suggest you get in touch with an attorney."

"I can't afford a lawyer," Michael said, extending his wrists, as the Sergeant applied the handcuffs.

"The court will appoint counsel," Van Eason assured him, motioning for another officer to step into the room and escort Michael out.

"I need to call my wife," Michael said.

"We'll let you take care of that," the Sergeant told him. "I don't let innocent people take the fall for crimes they didn't commit. I'm going to get you out of this."

"Thanks," the railroaded perp said before being led out into the corridor.

I could see that my old friend hated the thought of seeing a decent man being put through the jumps because of a creep like Trenton. He'd long suspected the arrogant thug of being connected, but no one had ever caught him in the act. This time an innocent man who'd already lost too much would bear the brunt of this mad man's hubris. That fact was not only tragic; it was unacceptable.

Roy wiped his face with his hands. "I know what you're thinking," he said to me.

"What?" I asked.

"You want to run a sting on Trenton. Well you can forget it, chump. That scorpion is poison and he's not going to let you get the goods on him twice. By the way, you never did tell me the whole story."

"A few years ago, Trenton was writing reviews for restaurants. He put a number of them out of business when he exposed rats and insects running through their kitchens. I later discovered that he was personally delivering the unwanted guests to the eateries. When I threatened to expose him, he sent some of his boys to change my mind. When enough of them ended up in the hospital with gunshot wounds, he stopped sending them.

"Trenton has obviously had bigger fish to fry since then, but I would never take that slimy character for granted. So you stay out of this."

"I'm not sure I can do that, Roy. Stewart could get locked up for a long time. Once he's gone, who'll look for his daughter?"

"You've got bigger problems."

"What do you mean?"

The Sergeant sighed and looked intently at me. "I didn't want to tell you until I knew for sure," he said. "But word on the street is that Pot Roast Sabastian has hired some muscle to take you out."

"I suppose he's still steaming about the trial," I concluded.

"I'd say it was a safe bet. You protected the witness who testified against his son. The kid got five years. Maybe I should provide some protection for you."

"That won't be necessary old friend. I'll call your boys in if things get too hot. Besides, tomorrow is going to be a very uneventful day. I'm just going to run a few errands and catch an old movie on television."

"Would one of those errands involve a certain young lady who works at the bank?"

"I've got to pay my bill, Roy."

"Right," he scoffed, as he opened the door and stopped. "I'm serious, Pete. There are a lot of monsters on the street and they're all gunning for you. Don't take any chances."

"I promise, Sarge," I said.

Though I would have been a fool to think Roy was uninformed, I didn't feel that I was in any immediate danger. After all, I'd managed to get through life with a skilled trigger finger and a miraculous instinct for avoiding trouble. To Roy, the miracle was that I'd actually lived this long.

CHAPTER 6

Even with Sergeant Van Eason's warnings echoing in the back of my mind, the day began on a rather pleasant note. I'd arrived at the First Citizen's Savings and Loan Bank to make the final payment on a chunk of change I borrowed a few months earlier. I needed the money to compensate an innocent bystander whose 1966 Mustang happened to be parked near the spot where I apprehended a bail jumper. While there's no need to go into detail, I will say it was the worst time for my brakes to fail. The vintage vehicle was totaled.

Despite how much I detested going into debt, I appreciated the importance of paying homage to such a fine machine. After all, I completely understood the relationship between an owner and a classic automobile. That historic piece of Americana was an intriguing symbol of simpler times and boundless dreams. It also belonged to the Mayor's wife.

Nevertheless, I'd paid my dues and hopefully improved the odds of getting my private investigator's license renewed. The only down side to this long awaited accomplishment was that I wouldn't have an excuse to visit my favorite loan officer, Brittany Truman. Brittany was a delightful lady with a warm disposition and a pair of ebony eyes that could make time stand still. It only took a glance at her spellbinding smile to make an aging bachelor forget he had an aching back and a job with no benefits.

Brittany and I were standing behind the teller's desk, looking over some forms she wanted me to sign. She was her usual perky self and I was just elated to be in the same room with her. She and a couple of tellers had come in to work a few minutes early. Our enjoyable exchange had me thinking about suggesting a celebratory dinner. Unfortunately, the three armed gorillas approaching the front entrance had other plans.

I didn't need a formal introduction to recognize the members of this demented trio. Like the rest of the city's most notorious hit men, their reputations preceded them.

The diminutive young man with the knotty dreadlocks and consistent snarl was Frankie "The Ninja" Sullivan. All decked out in black, this impudent malcontent took pride in the work he loved. Inflicting punishment was a skill he'd perfected with uncompromising precision. Though the third-degree black belt's hands were lethal weapons, his 9mm semiautomatic was indubitably more suited for the task at hand. This wasn't the first time I'd been the object of the Ninja's mordacity. Our last encounter ended with a bullet that left his older brother confined to a wheelchair. A lot of money was spent to arrange this unexpected reunion. Although personally, I think the little pipsqueak would've been happy to take me out for the cost of room and board.

Sullivan was accompanied by two of the most accomplished bruisers in the business. Mud Fish McClendon and Tsunami Nicholson were a two-man wrecking crew who would've knocked over a nine-year-old's lemonade stand if the price was right.

Deformed by the scars of a demoralized existence, McClendon appeared energized at the prospect of shedding blood. That maniacal grin revealed more about the curly-haired barbarian than merely a set of decaying teeth. This stocky degenerate loved to kill and he had no intention of leaving without his quarry.

Nicholson was just the opposite of his bloodthirsty compatriot. His nails and hair looked professionally maintained. The shine on those $300 shoes was practically blinding. There was no expression on his cleanly shaved pan. That black trench coat might have provided an air of respectability if it hadn't been used to conceal a 20 gauge pump action shot gun.

I had no doubt the militant morons were employed by the very racketeer Roy had warned me about before I left the police station. Pot Roast Sabastian was still steaming over his son's conviction and the vengeful gangster had gone to great lengths to make certain everyone involved with the trial felt his pain. I guess it was finally my turn.

Thanks to the efforts of a vindictive police inspector, I'd lost my permit to carry a semiautomatic. However, I was confident the 9-shot chamber of my 22LR revolver would be more than enough to withstand the impending offensive. My first inclination was to get Brittany and the tellers out of harm's way.

"What's going on?" Brittany frantically inquired when she saw my gun.

"Those guys are hired killers," I explained, pointing directly ahead. "Where are the others?"

"They're in the vault. What are we going to do?"

"Listen to me. I want you to calm down. Can you activate the alarm somewhere between here and the vault?"

"Yes."

"Once you've activated the alarm, the three of you need to get into the vault and stay in there. I know you have a mechanism in place for your protection."

"What about you?"

"I'll be alright," I assured her. "It's time to put an end to this."

After watching Brittany disappear through the glass doors to my far left, I turned my attention back to Sullivan, McClendon and Nicholson. As expected, Mud Fish was sporting the .44 Magnum that made him a legend. My safest bet was to take him out first.

When the gunmen entered the bank and spotted me taking cover behind the teller's desk, Sullivan opened fire. I held my position and planted a round into McClendon's shoulder.

When the psycho went down, Tsunami Nicholson splattered the walls with gunfire, destroying the printer and fax machine behind me!

The lobby wasn't well-lit, so Sullivan didn't notice the cardboard boxes of bottled water that had been collected for victims of the recent tornado. They were stacked in the open doorway of the office a few paces ahead of him. Never one to count the cost, the careless encroacher continued firing as he charged toward me! That's when I discharged three rounds into the boxes, wetting the floor beneath his feet. The Ninja slipped and collided with the wall, sustaining an injury to the knee on his way down!

As Sullivan took refuge inside the office, I exchanged a few more blasts with Tsunami Nicholson. I thought I had the situation well in hand until the victorious complacency of the rockets' red glare soon gave way to the methodizing chill of silent cannons. The last pathetic clicks from my empty revolver did little to curtail the madman's enthusiasm.

I opened one of the pouches strapped to my waist and pulled out a speed loader. I could hear the pounding of the man hunter's feet as he ambled forward. Triumph appeared in reach for Tsunami, but before he could claim his prize, the piercing wails of approaching sirens filled the air!

Just as a hunter anticipates a cornered animal's next move, I readily predicted Mud Fish and Tsunami's only option. They would need a hostage to get past the cops. That reality was all the incentive I needed. It was time to take a powder.

I stayed low until entering the narrow hallway which led to the rear exit. With my would-be captors otherwise preoccupied, I was convinced I'd given them the slip. I was wrong. I hadn't counted on the presence of a fourth attacker.

Awesome Anson English was a former professional wrestler who'd fallen on hard times. Like any other enterprising crime boss who depended upon the waning morals and resentful disposition of a desperate ex-con, Pot Roast Sabastian had worked swiftly to add this 400lb giant to the payroll.

Eternally obstinate and irreverently articulate, the massive brawler never missed an opportunity to make his position known. In extreme contrast to the persona his victims generally encountered, English was actually quite sophisticated. Before surrendering to the dark side, this seven foot destroyer was well respected by community leaders and politicians who praised him for his contributions to the betterment of society.

Even though the scarred bald head and tattooed biceps projected the character of an egregiously different person than most of his fans remembered, I still believed a repentant Awesome Anson was struggling to break free from the evil that had enslaved the big man's heart. Of course, a bullet riddled bank that had just been surrounded by the Police probably wasn't the best place to initiate a moment of self-evaluation.

I'd almost made it to the door when English emerged from the bathroom and caught me in a bear hug! I dropped my revolver and battled to loosen the rumbler's grip. Using every ounce of strength I could muster, I broke free and rammed his body into the wall with my shoulder, stifling the human dreadnought's momentum as he slid to the floor. I thought I'd taken the wind out of his sails, until he extended his leg and tripped me.

We both returned to our feet at the same time. Taking a cue from one of my favorite science fiction heroes, I surprised the towering hooligan with a flying kick to the chest! The force of his powerful frame sent me tumbling across the carpet. I raised my head in time to watch the clumsy behemoth land on his hips and roll over.

Neither of us appeared the picture of health, but I stumbled toward the rear exit and made another attempted at getting out of there in one piece.

I had the door open when English regained his footing and charged toward me. Before I could react, he tackled me through the doorway! We landed outside on the pavement where the infuriated gangster raised his hand and prepared to strike.

I would've been the first victim Awesome Anson English ever killed if the two uniformed police officers with M-16 rifles hadn't saved him from himself.

The cops cuffed the indignant goons' hands behind his back and led him away. I could hear him shouting as the authorities fought to maintain control.

"This is police brutality!" English declared. "That man attacked me. I was defending myself. I want my attorney. I know my rights!"

In retrospect, I suppose I should have asserted my contempt for a criminal conglomerate bent on shredding the moral fabric that held my community together. Instead, I just passed out.

CHAPTER 7

I awakened in the Emergency Room of Mount Sinai Memorial Hospital. My head was pounding and my ribs felt like I'd been hit by a Mack truck. I remembered telling a doctor that it only hurt when I laughed. That was actually a good thing since I couldn't find anything humorous about my present situation. With a face full of bruises, the silver lining behind every cloud was becoming more and more elusive. Yet, beneath the surface of man's most hideous experiences, there is often a surreal beacon of eternal optimism that makes life bearable once again. Mine was standing at the foot of the bed dressed in an olive-green business suit.

Between intervals of intercom pages and the routine movements of hospital personnel, I could hear the anguish in her husky voice. Even in my weakened condition, I couldn't deny the captivating aura of this shapely brunette. Though her dreamy brown eyes and pug nose projected the kind of dainty innocence that graced the pages of children's fairy tales, it didn't take long to realize that this extraordinary creature was more than just another pretty face. Moreover, considering what had happened the last time I made a woman the object of my affections, keeping my emotions in check and concentrating on the fee she could obviously afford to pay me appeared to be the best thing I could do for both of us.

"Mr. Masters," she said.

I pressed the button to raise the head of the bed. "Are you one of my doctors?" I groaned.

"No, my name is Mollie Fuller. I'm a friend of Michael Stewart."

"You must really be desperate to seek out a P. I. in the hospital."

"I've been looking for you all morning. When the policemen at the bank told me you'd gone to the hospital, it never occurred to me that you might be a patient. I'm sorry."

"No problem. How did you know to look for me at the bank?"

"I've been in the insurance game for twenty years, Mr. Masters. Over time, I've developed relationships with some of the best paid informants on the streets. There was one particular source that seemed to know more about you than all the others."

"Don't tell me. Her nose has been broken three times and that head of hair looks like the business end of a medieval torture device."

"That's the one. Database Della Maverick."

I really didn't have to ask the next question. Everyone looking to learn something about me received the same unflattering description from Database Della. I could quote it word for word. "What did she tell you about me?" I asked.

"She said you were a broad-shouldered brute with thick eyebrows and sideburns that made you look like an over-the-hill fifties rock star," Mollie relayed. "Now these are her words.

She said you dress like a gothic clown with no sense of color and style. You have an affinity for expensive black sneakers and you seldom wear a tie. She also had some unrepeatable opinions about your 1975 Plymouth Fury."

I partially smiled and shook my head. "What can I say?" I sighed. "It's nice to have fans. That woman has hated me for seven years."

"What did you do to her?"

"She ran a lucrative faith-healing scam until I blew the whistle on her. Now she panhandles and collects scraps from anyone who'll listen to her sad song...But I'm sure you didn't battle your way down here to rehash my old cases."

"No, I came to enlist your services. Michael Stewart is a former employee and a cherished friend. If you don't help him, I'm afraid he's going to be railroaded into prison."

I pointed to the chair in the corner. "Please sit down, Mrs. Fuller," I invited. "I've wanted to get involved with this case from the beginning, but the cops have vigorously declined my offer."

"I've been around a long time, Mr. Masters," Mollie said, sitting down. "I know there's a lot of politics hovering over a project with such a high profile. The police don't want to do anything the press can use to make them look bad. But letting Michael take the fall to stroke the ego of a man like Miles Trenton is outrageous. I know Michael. He's a loving father who would never do anything to hurt his child. The thought of him being accused of something so vile sickens me."

"If there's the slightest chance that Michael might be abusing his daughter, the State Attorney will be branded as the prosecutor who released a child molester back into the community."

"I know. That's why he won't give in on the gun charge."

"Have you spoken to Michael?" I asked.

"Yes," she replied. "He told me that you spoke up for him at the police station. You actually saw what Trenton was trying to do."

"He's right, but there was nothing incriminating on that monitor. It's just my word against Trenton's and he's very skilled at creating alternate realities."

"Just knowing you believe him means so much to Michael."

"When is his arraignment?"

"Tomorrow. If the judge grants bail, I should have him home by nightfall."

I was moved by Mollie's loyalty. A caring friend like her should never be denied. "I don't know how long I'll be in the hospital," I told her.

"I overheard one of the doctors say he was only going to keep you overnight for observation," she said.

"Maybe you should become a detective...Alright, Mrs. Fuller. As soon as I'm released, I'll have a chat with Sergeant Van Eason. If I make it out of his office alive, I'll see what I can do to help Michael."

"Thank you, Mr. Masters."

Despite my admiration for Mollie, I wasn't sure she understood what keeping Michael out of prison actually entailed. The concealed weapon charge wasn't going anywhere until the State Attorney was convinced his suspect didn't write that letter. I could only make that happen by either finding the person who did write it, or finding the missing girl. Regrettably, an entire police force with far more resources at its disposal had yet to accomplish that feat.

CHAPTER 8

After a long and restless night, I was released from the hospital with a fairly decent bill of health for a man my age. Of course, there was nothing decent about the exorbitant bill they expected me to pay. Nevertheless, I was grateful to be alive. According to the doctors, there was no permanent damage and I would be back to my old self in a couple of days.

As promised, I dropped in on my old pal Sergeant Roy Van Eason. Forever the professional, the devoted crime fighter was sitting at his desk behind a stack of personal effects his men had appropriated from the home of Michael Stewart. There wasn't a wrinkle in his navy blue uniform. The shine on those rubber soles was first rate. Even the four stripes on his lower sleeves were whiter than cotton. I couldn't imagine the pressure he was under. The last thing I wanted to do was make his situation worse, but I'd made a commitment to Mollie Fuller and I had to keep my word.

The Sergeant looked up and caught sight of me standing in the doorway. "Pete!" he exclaimed, rising from his seat and walking over to greet me. "When did you get out of the hospital?"

"A few hours ago," I told him.

"Come in and have a seat." He sat back down and retrieved my revolver from his desk drawer. "I thought you might want this back."

"I wondered what happened to it, but I didn't want to ask too many questions at the hospital," I said, taking possession of the weapon. "So what's the status on the freak brigade?"

"Tsunami Nicholson and Awesome Anson English are awaiting arraignment. Mud Fish McClendon is still in the hospital."

"What about Frankie Sullivan?"

"According to the officers at the scene, there were only three suspects."

"What?"

"No one saw Frankie Sullivan. He didn't even show up on the surveillance cameras."

I clutched my chin and sighed. "That little viper is on the loose and he won't be satisfied until he takes me out," I said. "Now I'm really going to be looking over my shoulder."

"Don't worry. We'll keep an extra eye open. At least you don't have to worry about trying to stay ahead of Sullivan and going head to head with Trenton at the same time."

I didn't want to bring up my conversation with Mollie Fuller, but it was time to come clean. "Well about that, Roy," I said.

The Sergeant could anticipate my next sentence. "Pete, please tell me you're not going to get involved with the Stewart case," he said.

"Stewart's friend, Mollie Fuller, hired me to clear his name. The poor guy needs all the help he can get. Even you don't believe he's guilty."

"You're right," he admitted, placing a stack of newspapers in front of me. "Each of these issues contains articles about the charitable acts Michael Stewart has performed for this community. This man has a stellar reputation and I don't believe he abused his daughter. But that's still no reason for you to sign up for a suicide mission."

"I know how you feel about this, Roy," I said. "I just can't stand to see a decent man take the fall for a snake like Trenton."

"Alright, Gumshoe," he conceded. "Keeping you busy might just be the best way to protect you. Considering these new developments, I'm going to need every available man."

"What new developments?" I asked.

Roy picked up a DVD and walked over to the television. "I've never seen anything like this," he said, switching the set on.

The shock in the Sergeant's eyes was justified. After fifteen years of investigating robberies, assaults and murders, I thought I'd witnessed every form of man's inhumanity to man. Yet, the DVD contained an aspect of child abuse that nearly brought me to tears.

The voice of a narrator began outlining the events we were witnessing. "This is a family business most parents wouldn't will to their children," he said. "State authorities have identified at least three families of jewel thieves and bank robbers who arm children as young as thirteen years of age. Security cameras detected these masked assailants committing crimes throughout the peninsula. So far, at least eight people have been killed in their wake."

Roy pressed the pause button. "I wouldn't care to see it a second time," he said.

"I don't blame you," I responded. "It's hard to believe there are parents who train their children to be armed thugs."

"Well, for some reason, Connie Stewart was obsessed with these people."

"Do you think she ran away to join up with one of these families?"

"It's hard to say. We only know of three, but there could be others. One of the families was apprehended this morning in Tampa. All of those kids were boys. From what we could gather from the security tapes, there were no girls involved in the other robberies either. However, the Department of Law Enforcement contacted me a few hours ago. They're investigating a jewelry store heist in Pensacola. This family's MO was a little different. They immediately located and spray-painted the security cameras. According to witnesses, they were in and out before the first police siren could be heard."

"How many?"

"There were six gunmen. The security guard swears the one with the revolver was female."

"Connie could be running with these weirdos," I said.

"Before she disappeared, the kid had started getting into trouble," Roy explained. "I don't suppose it would've taken a lot of wooing to draw her in."

"That's another thing. This was a nice girl from a law-abiding family. What could've provoked this infatuation with a band of outlaws?"

"Kids who surf the web have access to all kinds of mischief. Maybe she just stumbled across the site one day."

"It's possible, but I think someone provided a little help. Did she have many friends?"

"Her best friend was Mrs. Fuller's daughter, Karen. They spent a lot of time together. I didn't get a chance to interview her because they were out of town when everything went down. I didn't even realize who she was until she'd left the station and come looking for you."

"Did Karen give any indication how Connie might have learned about the robberies?"

"Connie had become very secretive. I'm sure there were a lot of things she kept to herself."

"Has anyone called in and reported seeing her?"

"No, but when Michael communicated online with who he thought was Clark Milford, the undercover officer quoted from passages she discovered in the predator's diary. It chronicled a day when Milford and Connie actually spoke. He recalled that Connie and a tall man with a ponytail were driving a Corvette. It didn't sound like the girl was in a hostage situation."

"How did Milford even get Connie's email address?" I wondered aloud.

"We found out that Milford used to be a custodian at Connie's school," Roy explained. "He was cleaning in one of the offices where she applied for some kind of contest. The guidelines required applicants to write down their email address. All the worm had to do was write it down."

"I'd still like to speak with Karen," I said as I stood up. "I'm going to stop by Mrs. Fuller's office and get her consent. But first, I'd like to have a talk with Michael Stewart. By the way, do you have anything else that might shed some light on the crime family's identity?"

"After two weeks of pounding the pavement, the boys in Robbery-Homicide have only come up with two names," he said, handing me a copy of the infamous letter that had gotten my client into so much trouble. "Jake Sasser and Paul Wright appear to be the assumed identities of choice."

"How do you know they're assumed names?" I asked, perusing the letter.

"Sasser and Wright were prominent business men in this town."

"Shouldn't someone talk to them?"

"We can't. They've been dead for forty years."

I placed the letter on the desk and sighed. "These thieves are really good," I commented. "Trenton is no slouch either."

"After that job in Pensacola, it would be wise for the family of robbers to lay low for a while," Roy concluded. "However, if you do find Connie with them, I doubt they'll give her up without a fight. So be careful."

"You bet."

"I'm serious, Pete. Even if you didn't have to worry about our gang of robbers, or the scores of criminals who want to see you dead; Trenton is still out there. He didn't set Michael Stewart up to hone his skills. That piece of slime has a plan. If you get in his way, he won't hesitate to dump your bionic carcass into the Chipola River."

"Don't worry, old pal," I said with a smile. "I've got eyes in the back of my head."

I knew my putrid attempt at levity didn't do much to ease the Sergeant's mind. His vigilance was warranted. If someone did infiltrate Michael Stewart's world to seduce his daughter into a life of crime, I could soon find myself facing a syndicate of armed bandits. At any rate, I was thankful for Roy's concern. Friendship like his was something money couldn't buy. I certainly didn't want him to think I didn't take his regard for my welfare seriously. I'd always had a tendency to make jokes when I didn't want to admit I was afraid. Despite this missing link in the chain of my emotional development, I was mature enough to realize how dangerous it was to take a man like Miles Trenton for granted. Even if I did have eyes in the back of my head, that skunk would've paid somebody to put them out.

CHAPTER 9

Sooner or later, certain men encounter that inevitable moment when they are compelled to challenge the guiding principles so many have embraced without question. With no intention of straying from the path of moral enlightenment, these disconcerted individuals seek to understand the indiscriminate calamities that can alter the course of a kind and caring spirit. For Michael Stewart, the odyssey was just beginning.

Michael's contemporary suburban home was an earnest tribute to the values his father's generation once held dear. The picturesque lawn looked regularly maintained. Symmetrically trimmed hedges along the front of the house were well-watered and healthy. There was an image of praying hands on the welcome mat. I halfway expected a little boy in cuffed dungarees and a baseball cap to come running past me. Even the lilies along the asphalt driveway seemed to reflect the heart of this personable gentleman who'd worked so hard to set a meaningful example for his family.

Without a doubt, Michael Stewart had spent his life playing by the rules and believing he would cross the finish line with his head held high. Now, it looked as though the champions were being stripped of their glory while the cheaters walked away with the gold.

When Michael's wife, Maxine, answered the door, she appeared frightened and exhausted. Those somber brown eyes had shed a lot of tears in the past twenty-four hours. Yet, she was willing to endure it all for the most amazing man she'd ever known.

Though I'd only heard bits and pieces of their remarkable story, I had to conclude that the love of a woman like this didn't come along every day.

She emerged during the most treacherous days of Michael's life. His first wife, Delta, was dying. Even then the shadows of morbid discontent weren't able to eclipse the glimmer of hope in the loving husband's eyes. That was when Maxine changed his world forever.

In their bleakest hour of need, the statuesque brunette with the incandescent smile became the rock upon which the Stewarts came to lean. The veteran health care professional didn't hesitate to put her training to good use when Delta succumbed to the viciousness of an unexplainable disease.

After the death of the first Mrs. Stewart, the friendship between Michael and Maxine blossomed into a romance. A year later, they were married.

Their union was only two years old, but the ups and downs of adjusting to a new dynamic didn't diminish the passion they felt for one another. To these newlyweds, nothing was strong enough to destroy their love. Of course, that was before either of them had ever experienced the loss of a child.

Shortly after Connie's disappearance, Maxine and Michael found themselves taking their frustrations out on each other.

Maxine had only known her stepdaughter for a short time. Yet, she and Connie had forged a bond that defied the territorial conflicts of most blended families. Blinded by the scattered debris of his own grief, Michael failed to see the anguish that deformed his wife's temperament.

While she could appreciate the emptiness and sense of failure her husband was enduring, Maxine couldn't get past the rejection she felt when he'd choose to retreat into an abyss of secluded sadness.

Michael had opted for early retirement, reckoning the time spent at home would afford him the emotional edification he needed to repair his broken family. Tragically, there could be no restoration until every member of the household was in place.

"Come in, Mr. Masters," the lady of the house said. "We were so happy to receive your call. Thank you for taking Michael's case."

"You're quite welcome, Mrs. Stewart," I replied. "I'm going to do everything I can to help your husband and bring Connie home."

She led me into the living room where Michael was sitting in front of the television with a glass of tea in his hand. He was watching the news.

"Local authorities aren't releasing any information about the incident that took place at this house on Boliva Road two days ago," the reporter said. "Our sources tell us that while the cameras were turned off, an unidentified suspect was taken into custody. Of course, this was alleged to have occurred during the taping of Miles Trenton's Internet Predator feature. None of our colleagues at Channel 16 had any comment. We also tried to speak with the head of the Police Department's Internet Predator Task Force, Sergeant Roy Van Eason, but he declined to be interviewed. I'm Bart Mavis. For more on this story as well as the situation with the forest fires throughout Southern Georgia and the Panhandle, stay tuned to this station."

"Mr. Masters is here, honey," Maxine told Michael.

My fatigued client stood up and extended his hand. "Good to see you again, Mr. Masters," he said. "Thank you for coming. Please sit down."

I took a seat in the recliner as Maxine poured me a glass of tea and joined her husband on the couch. Michael picked up the remote and switched off the television.

"I must admit this is one of the most unusual cases I've ever run across," I told them. "On the other hand, when Miles Trenton is involved, anything is possible."

"So this isn't the first time you've seen him in action," Michael said, taking a sip from his glass. "I'm not surprised. The man's a snake. He'll do anything to promote his own interest."

"I couldn't agree more," I said. "But we're going to need a lot more than a trip into the bathroom with his cell phone to bring him down."

"When I saw that smug liar, I was overcome with the memories of all he'd done to so many innocent people," Michael explained. "I guess I didn't think about how far he was willing to go to get even."

"I saw the letter," I said.

"It's a vicious lie!" Maxine declared. "My husband is a loving father who'd never do anything to hurt his child. Connie would tell you the same thing."

"Maybe," Michael muttered.

"What do you mean?" she asked.

"Before she disappeared, Connie became someone I didn't recognize," the tearful father recalled. "I don't know what she would say about me now."

Maxine put her arm around her husband and kissed him on the forehead.

Dreading the truth that had to be revealed, I lowered my head and breathed heavily. "I'm afraid you won't like what I've already learned," I said.

Michael leaned forward. "I'd rather hear it now," he said.

"Based on some of the items found among Connie's personal possessions, Sergeant Van Eason has reason to believe she might have reached out to a family of armed robbers," I continued. "Their most recent heists have occurred in the Panhandle. So there's a good chance the child hasn't ventured far from home."

Michael squinted and shook his head. "It just keeps getting worse," he lamented.

"But how could she have gotten involved with these people?" the puzzled stepmother wondered aloud.

"I have a few theories," I replied. "She could have learned about them through schoolmates or read something that piqued her curiosity. It's also possible that some enemies of yours could've orchestrated a conspiracy just to make you suffer. Can you think of anyone who might hate the two of you enough to lure your daughter into an underworld of criminal activity?"

"I can think of one person," Michael responded. "His name is Tim Herbert. He's a vindictive little maggot who blames me for the death of Ann Kester."

"Ann Kester?" I replied.

"She was Mollie's secretary," he explained. "After breaking up with her boyfriend, Ann turned to me for comfort. I thought of her as a little sister, but her feelings ran much deeper. I had no idea until the detective who investigated her suicide informed me that she had written it all down in her diary. I'll never forgive myself for not recognizing the signs."

"You couldn't have known," Maxine told him.

"Do the names Jake Sasser or Paul Wright mean anything to either one of you?" I asked.

"I don't think I've ever heard those names," Michael said.

"Neither have I," Maxine concurred, checking her watch. "I'm sorry, but I have to be going."

"That's right," her husband remembered, as the two of them stood up. "My wife is a very dedicated nurse, Mr. Masters. She has to work extra hours because so many of her co-workers have been affected by the forest fires."

They kissed. "I'll be back as soon as I can," Maxine promised. "Don't worry. We've finally got the help we need." She turned to me. "Mr. Masters, thank you again for helping us."

"I'm going to do everything I can, Mrs. Stewart," I said, rising to take her hand.

When Maxine left, Michael and I sat back down. "You have a lot of people in your life who love you, Mr. Stewart," I observed.

"No man could ask for a more loving and devoted wife," he said. "When I think about the stupid fight we had the night before I was arrested, I could crawl under a rock. She'd always dreaded the thought of us spending time apart, but when she walked out of here that morning, I think she was looking forward to every minute. Maxine is the best and I don't ever want to do anything that would cost me her love."

"Mrs. Fuller seems to care about you as well."

"Oh yes. Mollie was my supervisor when I retired from the insurance agency. She has always been a true friend and I'm going to pay back every penny she's spent in my behalf."

I noticed a change in his facial expression. "Is there something else you'd like to discuss?" I inquired.

"Everything just seems so out of balance," he said. "There was a time when a man who tried to live a good life and treat others the way he wanted to be treated could expect something better."

I didn't want to make matters worse by spouting some irrelevant cliché, but I felt the need to say something. "Mr. Stewart, I can't put myself in your place and I'm certainly in no position to counsel you," I told him. "However, I do know something about tragedy and loss. I've seen incredibly solicitous people go through the most devastating anguish you can imagine."

"I believe you. Don't get me wrong, Masters. I'm not delusional. I know there are people who've overcome more than I'll ever face. It's just that I can't help wondering if all the good deeds I've done weren't in vain."

"Well I don't know that much about you, but I have learned that the lives of many people have been enriched by your generosity. That's an extraordinary legacy."

"Does it really mean anything?"

"Yes, it does. Despite everything you and your daughter have experienced, the values you've taught her are still somewhere in the depths of her heart. She may be on the wrong path for the moment, but at some point she will come to her senses and remember the kind of person you wanted her to become. That's worth more than all the money in the world."

"I know you're right, but it's so hard to see right now. My life is a mess. You heard what that reporter said. Miles Trenton is keeping his mouth shut. That parasite is going to let the scandal blow up without lifting a finger. I'll be ruined and he'll look like the hero journalist who did everything he could to protect the twisted father who had everybody fooled. No one will be able to say he manipulated the facts. The man's a menace."

I reached into my pocket for a business card. "I'm not going to let the likes of Miles Trenton destroy your reputation," I assured him. "By the way, I'll need a recent picture of Connie."

Michael stood up and pulled out his wallet. "I don't care what happens to me anymore," he said, slipping the photo out and handing it to me. "Just bring my little girl home."

"I'm going to do everything I can."

"Thank you."

I left the Stewart home wishing I could have been more encouraging. Michael was clearly a loving father who'd done all he could to better the lives of everyone around him. Sadly, even the most charitable soul must battle the malevolence of an imperfect world. I wasn't privy to every trauma this endearing man had suffered, but our conversation revealed he definitely had enemies. If the road to finding his daughter was about to lead me through a labyrinth of lies and treachery, I would need to explore the darkness beneath the shadows of their intentions before I could begin the journey.

CHAPTER 10

After the ringing endorsement Database Della Maverick had given me, I didn't suspect Mollie Fuller would be too disturbed by my somewhat eccentric appearance when I arrived at the Lincoln Porter Insurance Agency. While there was no question the startled occupants of the desks stationed just outside the supervisor's office would have preferred to see me properly attired in a traditional suit and tie, I felt the urgency of the moment called for me to worry more about getting the job done than attempting to make a fashion statement. So without reservation, I stepped off the elevator in a pair of solid brown khakis and a midnight blue blazer that exquisitely complemented my $150 jet-black running sneakers.

I realized a few of these pretentious social climbers were taken aback by the sight of an uncultured gumshoe with no regard for the archaic convention that defined their world. They had no idea that in my line of work, the right bullet at the wrong time could make the entire discussion seem rather moot.

In spite of the less than cordial welcome, I confidently approached my client's office. I'd called ahead to let her know I was on my way, so when I knocked on the door she immediately ushered me in.

Like Mollie, the office was warm and unassuming. Her well-arranged desk looked a little rough around the edges. A portrait of her late husband hung amid her numerous degrees and a collection of her daughter's academic accomplishments. A set of smaller photos atop the table by the window served as framed reminders of a time that seemed so far away. There were days when the memories could be crippling. Yet, in the midst of her despair, she'd always mustered the courage to be grateful for the treasures that still remained.

"Sit down, Mr. Masters," Mollie invited, walking back around her desk to take a seat. "I have to admit I was surprised to hear you suggest that someone with a vendetta against Michael might have had something to do with what happened to Connie."

"I'm just trying to approach the situation from every conceivable angle," I explained, reaching into my pocket for a slip of paper. "This list of enemies you recited over the telephone contains one name Michael mentioned when I was at his home."

"Let me guess...Tim Herbert."

"Exactly...What's the story between those two?"

She looked back and shook her head. "Where do I begin?" she sighed. "Their feud took root about a year ago when Ann Kester broke up with her boyfriend."

"Michael told me about her," I said. "She was your secretary."

"That's right."

"He also said she killed herself."

"That's true, but she had more problems than even Michael realized. Ann suffered from Fibromyalgia. I was the only one at work who knew and I kept her secret till the day she died. In fact, you're the only other person I've ever told."

"Did she end her life because she had the Fibromyalgia, or did her feelings for Michael send her over the edge?"

"Oh, I'm sure it was a combination of the two. Though there were no visible signs of her ailment, the poor woman was in pain twenty-four hours a day. I don't know how she managed to come to work at all. Toward the end, she started missing days. I knew it was just a matter of time before she'd have to let the job go. I never expected her to take her own life."

"I presume Tim Herbert's affections were not reciprocated."

"You're right," she said, wiping a tear from her eye. "That kid fawned over her like a lovesick puppy. I'm not sure she even knew how he felt, but when Ann turned to Michael, Tim blew a gasket."

"Where can I find Mr. Herbert?"

"He'll be spending most of his time in accounting until the tax season is over."

"What can you tell me about Joe Fisher?"

"He's just an old dinosaur who has trouble adapting to change. He and Michael have butted heads a few times in the past, but that's just the old goat's way. He's really harmless."

"I'd like to talk to him."

"You'll have to wait until he returns from the police station."

"The police station?" I repeated.

"Yes, a couple of officers came in this morning and asked him to accompany them downtown," she said.

"Did they arrest him?"

"No, they just wanted him to come down and answer a few questions. I assumed it had something to do with one of his cases."

Though I was very interested in finding out why the cops were questioning Fisher, I didn't want to leave without talking to Tim Herbert. I also intended to interview the one person who knew Connie better than anyone.

Reluctant to bring up the primary reason why I'd come, I paused for a moment and looked toward the window. "I need to speak with Karen," I said.

"I know," Mollie acknowledged, rising from her seat. "She should be arriving within thirty minutes. I'm going down to the lobby to meet her. She's a shy and self-conscious girl. I want her to be prepared for your meeting."

"Don't worry, Mrs. Fuller," I said, as I stood up. "I've been in this business for a while. I'm not going to say or do anything to hurt your daughter."

"I appreciate that."

"By the way," I said, before she made it to the door. "Have any new employees been hired in the past few months?"

"The only one I can think of is Chuck Wheeler," she said. "He's been one of our custodians for the past eleven months."

"Thank you, Mrs. Fuller."

The chamber of misery behind Mollie's eyes hadn't impeded her propensity for loving the people in her life. She didn't have to tell me how much she adored her daughter. The sentiment was written all over her face. Karen was very precious to her mother and I had every intention of handling that treasure with care.

CHAPTER 11

I had no idea how long it would take Mollie to return with Karen and I didn't want to waste valuable time waiting around in the office. So I decided to venture out and make my way to accounting. I'd almost reached the door when an auburn-haired malcontent came trudging in with a mail cart.

Her name was Jodie Parker. For the past twenty-six years, this resentful smart aleck had toiled diligently in the mail room while watching the interns she'd trained move on to bigger and better things.

Though she often asserted that a veteran like herself didn't have a chance because younger women were getting by on their youth and beauty, Jodie was quite attractive in her own right. She was tall and full-figured. That burgundy pant suit gave her an air of incredible distinction. Unfortunately, a shroud of insolence that impelled her to blame the world for all her problems, made it virtually impossible for others to identify the deep-seated integrity that was dying to come out.

"Good morning," I said.

"That's your opinion," she responded, going about her work as if I weren't in the room.

"My name is Masters. I'm a private investigator."

"Congratulations."

"I was hired to find Michael Stewart's missing daughter."

That little piece of information seemed to soften her demeanor. "Michael's a good man," she said. "He doesn't deserve the lousy things that have happened to him."

"There has been speculation that she might have run away from home."

"I heard."

"How well do you know Michael?"

"Well enough to know he'd do anything for his child."

"You really think a lot of him."

"He's one of the few people who never let me down," she confessed, as she walked over to the window and stared down at the traffic. "I've never had a great social network, Masters. Even the people who were supposed to love and protect me turned out to be soulless savages. That kind of mistreatment sets the stage for a very troubled life. You start off trusting everything and everyone until your heart gets trampled beyond recognition. After that, you just put up a wall and shut down."

"I'm sorry," I said. "I didn't mean to upset you."

"I'm not upset. I just want you to understand how gratifying it is for someone who came up the way I did to be around a man like Michael. He's a decent man who always tries to do the right thing."

"I understand there's someone who might disagree with that assessment."

"Oh, don't get me started on that little squirt! Tim Herbert may be an accounting genius, but when it comes to real life, that boy has all the common sense of a sponge."

"I was told that the suicide of Ann Kester was the reason for Tim's animosity."

For the first time this hardened survivor seemed unable to conceal her vulnerability. "You really do know your stuff," she said. "I loved Ann like a daughter. She was the closest thing to a loving family that I'll ever know. I can still see that genuine smile reflecting the sincere compassion she felt for everyone. She wasn't like these sugar and spice little harpies who sell their self-respect to the highest bidder. Ann had real class. We could disagree without fighting. Even though the child wore more makeup than a clown, I thought it was a rule of society that forced women to conform to an impossible standard." She studied my expression. "You don't agree."

"It's not a subject I've spent much time pondering over," I said.

"That's the kind of diplomatic answer Ann would've given."

"I know this isn't easy to talk about, but I have to ask these questions. Do you think Tim Herbert hated Michael enough to lure his daughter away from home?"

"That nitwit couldn't lure a starving vulture to a dead rhino. Besides, he's no criminal. He's an idiot, but he's no criminal. He just had it bad for Ann. I couldn't fault any man for that."

"She must've been very special."

"She was the best."

Neither of us spoke another word as Jodie retrieved the remaining pieces of mail from her cart and placed them on the desk before solemnly taking her leave.

I grappled for the words that would bring comfort to this complicated lady, but the burden of sorrow was far too cumbersome for trite expressions and worn out platitudes. She was a woman in mourning. Although she and Ann didn't share the same DNA, Jodie felt a void that would afflict her for the rest of her life. In every way that mattered, she had suffered the loss of a child and nothing I could say or do would ever erase that pain.

CHAPTER 12

The atmosphere in accounting was more chaotic than I'd anticipated. People were literally running down the corridors with calculators and receipts for every transaction made since the Korean War.

A few were standing in their office doorways, shouting figures at each other. Telephone conversations were loud and abrasive. Antacids made the rounds like candy. Amid this alarming state of anarchy, I could barely hear myself think. I couldn't imagine how anyone could conduct business in such a mad house. That's why I was so astonished to find Tim Herbert sitting calmly with his feet up, while the mellow tones of jazz piano filled the office.

After the monstrous description I'd gotten from Michael and Jodie, I expected the twenty-six year old mathematics wizard to be bigger than life. Yet, at six-feet-two-inches tall, he looked practically gaunt. He had a tiny mole on the side of his chin and that flattop haircut resembled and overused scouring pad. In my mind, I struggled to compose an image of this displaced loner with the horn-rimmed glasses confronting Michael Stewart in a jealous rage, but the film just wouldn't develop. Nevertheless, I needed to hear his story.

As one would expect, the unexplainable quirks of this imaginative genius weren't confined to his appearance. The condition of his office made that fact abundantly clear.

Stacks of documents were scattered across the floor. Enormous legal and economic reference volumes occupied the sitting space of that black leather couch to my right. The potted plant near the door hadn't been watered in days. I didn't see how an individual who had to work in that environment could maintain his sanity. When I looked across the room and beheld the little table where framed photos of Ann Kester allowed this lonely young man to relive the happiest moments of his life, I didn't have to wonder anymore.

"Mr. Herbert," I said, knocking at his open door.

Fearing he'd been surprised by the brass, the rattled bean counter jumped out of his chair and ran over to switch off the stereo! "Yes, I'm Tim Herbert," he said, adjusting his tie. "What can I do for you?"

"My name is Masters. I'm looking into the disappearance of Michael Stewart's daughter."

The mention of Michael's name seemed to drain the energy from Herbert's body. "I see," he grunted, pointing to the chair in front of his desk as he sat down. "Please have a seat, Mr. Masters."

"I understand you and Michael weren't on the best of terms," I said, sitting down.

"That's putting it mildly. Michael Stewart is a conniving worm who'd do anything to get what he wants."

"Do you think he manipulated Ann Kester?"

He lowered his head. "I guess I shouldn't be surprised at that question," he said. "Everyone knows how much I loved her. I just don't understand what she saw in him."

"Did you have occasion to speak with his daughter?"

He thought for a moment. "Hey, wait a minute!" he insisted. "I hope you're not suggesting I had something to do with that kid's disappearance."

"Did you?" I asked him.

"No!" he responded, springing to his feet. Realizing his temper was about to get the best of him, he took a breath and walked over to the table where Ann's pictures were displayed. Struggling to contain himself, the bereaved dreamer touched one of the photos. "This was the last time I saw her," he said. "We were at a charity banquet. When she didn't come to work the next day, I assumed she was just taking some personal time. A week later, she committed suicide."

I gently approached him and looked at the photographs. One of them immediately caught my attention. It was a picture of Mollie, Jodie and Ann standing in front of an ice sculpture.

I was especially intrigued with the brooch Jodie was wearing. The amazing piece of jewelry was a white bird cameo against a sepia stone set in filigree gold. "That's quite a pin Ms. Parker is wearing," I commented.

"People gawked at it all night," Herbert replied, taking off his glasses and wiping his eyes. "I asked her where she got it, but the old bat wasn't volunteering any information."

I looked at him one last time. "Mr. Herbert, I didn't come here to manipulate you and I'm not trying to make you cop to something you didn't do. That's not the way I do business. So I'm going to ask you straight out. Did you have anything to do with Connie Stewart's disappearance?"

Herbert clutched his face with his hands and glanced up at the ceiling before putting his glasses back on. "At Ann's memorial service, I got loaded and took a swing at Michael," he confessed. "It was a stupid thing to do, but I felt justified. The woman I adored was gone and she'd spent her last precious days pining for a man who'd married someone else. I made a fool of myself. When people go out of their way to let you know you don't belong, you grow up praying for a caring friend who'll give you a fair chance. A woman like Ann made an awkward boy with glasses feel like he'd finally found that special girl who would make his dreams come true. It's not easy admitting I got caught up in a child's fantasy."

I placed my hand to my mouth and looked at the floor. "I don't know what to say, Mr. Herbert," I told him.

"You're a kind man, Mr. Masters, but you didn't come all this way to hear me lament. I've never liked Michael Stewart and we'll never be friends, but I didn't harm his teenage daughter. I'd never do that."

It might have been the empathy I felt for this mercurial young man that softened my opinion. Or it was possibly the bond I shared with every misdirected soul who'd ever nursed a broken heart. At any rate, I believed his story. He'd been more than forthcoming about the animosity he felt for Michael and he was beginning to understand the self-deceiving infatuation that compelled him to expect more from Ann than she had to give. Coming to terms with his mistakes and procuring a measure of inner peace would be the final victory. It would also prove to be the most grueling, because success depended upon his ability to be honest with the man in the mirror. So far, that consistent accuser had been the most malicious opposer in Tim Herbert's life.

CHAPTER 13

By the time I made it back to Mollie's floor, she'd returned with her daughter, Karen. The two of them were waiting for me in the conference room.

It didn't take a detective to recognize the love Mollie felt for this remarkable young lady.

With every touch the depth of her devotion was made manifest. I had no doubt that this benevolent protector watched over her child with unyielding vigilance. That's why I was so surprised when she stood up to leave.

"You have every right to be present, Mrs. Fuller," I said.

"I know," she whispered. "But there may be something you need to know that she's not ready to share with me. Besides, I believe you're the kind of man I can trust."

I appreciated Mollie's faith in my compassion and professionalism. I wasn't used to having clients feel so comfortable with me in the beginning. I guess one of the advantages of being an eccentric in the wake of catastrophe was that people generally deemed it wiser to put up with me than confront the alternative.

The child was obviously uncomfortable. She'd borne the shackles of fear and guilt since the day Connie vanished. Though Karen was mentally capable of understanding that her friend's disappearance wasn't her fault, pangs of contrition plagued her conscience like a swarm of locusts.

That's the way it had always been with this burgeoning scholar. Even within the confines of adolescent perceptions, she seemed to embody the warmth and compassion to which so many had failed to aspire. In spite of the cruelty and dejection that clouded her existence, this exceptional teenager wouldn't allow the scourge of bitterness to define her character. Those who chose to look past the outer appearance and embrace the princess she was inside were never disappointed. Loving too much and weighing more than most of society considered beautiful was her only infraction. For evading the pitfalls that had derailed countless young lives, she'd been sentenced to a life in a dungeon of teenage ostracism. From where I stood, that was the real crime.

"Karen, this is Mr. Masters," Mollie said. "He's the private investigator I mentioned. I want you to be completely honest with him. It's the only way he'll be able to find Connie and help Mr. Stewart. This is very important, honey."

"I know, Mom," she responded.

When her mother left, I pulled a chair from the huge conference table and sat down beside Karen. She was wearing a midnight blue blazer with the debate team logo. I could see she was no average kid. So I made up my mind to play it straight with her from the start.

"Your mother really looks out for you," I commented.

"She thinks I'm still a baby."

"She just wants the best for you. I wouldn't take it for granted."

"I guess you're going to tell me I'll appreciate it when I'm older."

"You'll see."

She looked at me as though her heart was about to break. "Do you think Connie's dead?" she asked.

"I don't know," I said. "There's so much about this case that doesn't make sense. No one has contacted the family for ransom. Until recently, Connie was just a decent kid doing the best she could. What could've happened? Did she suffer some kind of emotional trauma? Do you have any ideas?"

Karen turned away and peered at the wall. "It's my fault," she muttered.

"What do you mean?"

"I was afraid to tell Mr. Stewart."

"What do you know, girl?"

"I just wanted to meet him, but I was too shy."

"Who did you want to meet?"

"Chuck."

"Chuck Wheeler?"

"Yes," she replied. "I thought he was cute. So I asked Connie to get to know him and introduce us. She wasn't afraid of anybody."

"How old is Chuck?" I asked.

"I think he's twenty-four."

"How far did things get?"

"We finally met, but I could see he wasn't interested."

"How did he feel about Connie?"

A look of torturous confusion swept over the teenager's face as she placed her hands to her head. "He and Connie really got close," she said, struggling to fight back tears. "When I'd come here to meet her after school, she and Chuck would be having a grand ole time. She said they were just friends. I wanted to believe her, but something just didn't feel right."

Choosing my words carefully, I leaned closer and lowered my voice. "Do you think anything else might have happened between the two of them?" I asked.

"If you'd asked me that a year ago, I would've said no. Connie and I had big plans for the future. Neither of us wanted to ruin them by getting into trouble. I really thought I knew her, but so much has changed. I honestly couldn't tell you anything for certain."

I sensed there was something she was leaving out. "Karen, did you and Connie have a fight?" I inquired.

"Yes," she responded, nodding her head as she burst into tears. "I was mad because Chuck liked her instead of me. I called her a backstabbing lowlife. I didn't know she was going to turn up missing. I wish I could take it all back."

"None of this is your doing, kid," I told her. "We all say things we don't mean. You've got to forgive yourself."

"My daddy was like you. There was nothing I couldn't tell him when he was alive. I miss him so much."

"Your mother would like for you to confide in her, too. She really loves you."

"I know, but we live in different worlds. Mom is beautiful. She doesn't know how it feels to hear guys make animal noises when she walks by. She's never cried herself to sleep because some girl taped an ugly drawing to the bulletin board and wrote her name underneath. She's stylish and confident. I'll never be like her."

"Have you told her how you feel?"

"She wouldn't understand."

"I think she would," I said, directing the girl's attention toward the sobbing mother standing in the doorway.

Karen got up and ran to her. "Mom," she whispered.

"It's alright, baby," Mollie said, as she embraced her daughter. "I didn't know. Please forgive me."

There are times when the silence can be more deafening than the tumultuous pounding of a terrified heart. Daunted by the dread of being judged by the only person she had left in this world, Karen had spent the most difficult time in a teenager's life concealing the scars of a tormented spirit. Now that the truth was out, this extraordinary young woman would no longer feel the need to bear her burdens alone.

CHAPTER 14

While I was pleased to have played a part in the renewing of Karen and Mollie's relationship, my conversation with the teen hadn't brought anything mind-blowing to light. However, I was quite intrigued to hear about the friendship that existed between Chuck Wheeler and the missing girl. Although I was fully aware of what can happen when an investigator gets lost beneath a fog of preconceived notions, I couldn't stop wondering what a twenty-four year old man had in common with a teenage girl. I would only learn the answer by asking him face to face.

I caught sight of the young custodian as he approached the hot dog stand a few yards down the street from the agency building. He was tall, muscular and good-looking. His visage was grim. There was definitely something ugly lurking behind those rueful green eyes. Yet, he was warm and engaging. His ability to intelligently express himself made it obvious that he was nobody's fool. The casual observer would likely have presumed this kid was on a fast track to a prosperous future. I just hoped it didn't include a stint in the big house for having an inappropriate relationship with a minor.

Given the choice, I'd rather have spoken to Mr. Wheeler in a more desirable setting. The noon hour traffic was bustling and the smell of smoke from the forest fires near Tallahassee filled the air. Even the mild temperature and bright sunshine didn't calm the tempers of impatient motorists who yearned to be heard.

Wheeler was wiping a stain from the sleeve of his charcoal gray coveralls when he looked up and saw me. I could see why a young girl would find him so appealing. That silky black ducktail must've made Connie and Karen's adolescent hearts quiver.

"Chuck Wheeler?" I shouted above the noise of a passing truck.

"I'm Wheeler," he responded.

"My name is Masters. I'm a private investigator. I was hired to find Michael Stewart's missing daughter."

"So it is true," he said, taking a bite of his hot dog as we walked over to a bench and sat down.

"What's true?" I asked.

"I heard through the office grapevine that Mollie Fuller was bringing in a P.I. to help find Mr. Stewart's daughter."

"Do you know Michael well?"

"No, I've only been on the job a little less than a year. I didn't have many conversations with him before he retired, but I did hear that he was a decent guy."

"Is that what Connie told you?"

He looked down and rubbed his chin. "I suppose someone has been filling your head with deplorable stories about me and that little girl," he concluded.

"Not at all," I assured him. "I was merely told that you and Connie spent time together."

"That's right. She and I did talk a few times. She used to tell me about her problems at home."

"Did she ever give any indication that she wanted to run away?"

"No."

"Was she afraid of anyone?"

"Not to my knowledge."

"What did she tell you about her father?"

"Just the usual teenage drama. She didn't think Mr. Stewart understood her. She wanted to get a tattoo, but she knew he wouldn't approve."

"Did she ever say he mistreated her in anyway?"

"No, but she did say he hadn't been the same since the Kester woman died."

"Did you ever meet Ann Kester?"

"No."

"That tragedy seemed to touch a lot of the employees of this agency," I commented.

"I gathered that, too," he said. "It was all people talked about for the longest time."

"What did they say?"

"Nothing that wasn't common knowledge. They mentioned how sad she looked and how she'd started to miss work toward the end."

"Did anyone say how she died?"

"I heard she just swallowed a bottle of Pregabalin and ended it all."

I was about to engage him further when a lady with a baby carriage stepped into the path of an oncoming motorcycle! The two of us leaped to our feet, intending to render assistance, but the startled pedestrian was on the other side of the street. Fortunately, she had the presence of mind to snatch her child from the jaws of certain death before the speeding vehicle could reach them.

"That was a close one," Wheeler gasped.

"Too close," I added.

Once I regained my composure, I sat back down and watched the passing cars. Without saying a word, Wheeler joined me.

"I know what you want to ask me," the young man said. "And the answer is "no." I didn't touch Connie."

"Do you know where she could've gone?"

"I don't have a clue. I'm not into teenage girls, Mr. Masters. You can check me out. I don't have a record. I was just an adult with a listening ear."

"Alright, Mr. Wheeler," I said, rising to shake his hand. "Thank you for your time."

While I wouldn't have declared my interviews with Michael's co-workers a complete waste of time, the explanations they provided were hardly the kind of indisputable evidence I needed to clear my client's name. I was certainly no closer to finding his missing daughter. For the time being, it looked as though I'd have to table my vendetta theory and concentrate on a more plausible plan of action. On the other hand, I'd yet to hear what Joe Fisher had to tell me.

CHAPTER 15

More than a decade of endeavoring to understand the criminal mind hadn't prepared me for the cataclysmic phenomenon who answered to the name of Joe Fisher. Though I'd read detective mysteries and watched classic movies that featured old-school tough guys who weren't afraid of anything, I never expected to meet one in person.

Everything about this insolent retired cop embodied the abrasive fearlessness of days gone by. Even his plain brown suit and fedora looked intimidating. The lines on his battered mug exposed the remnants of a consciousness consumed by loss and regret. That huge bulbous nose had obviously been broken a few times. Despite the callous comportment, the disconcerting manner in which he clutched his age-blotched hands atop the table told me this apathetic hardball that time forgot had something to hide.

Fisher remained silent as he watched Sergeant Van Eason and me enter the interrogation room. Though he was gravely concerned about the file Roy had tucked under his arm, the defiant ruffian didn't want us to see him sweat.

"I suppose you know why you've been detained," Roy said.

"I don't know anything," Fisher responded.

"This is Pete Masters," the Sergeant said. "He's also an investigator."

"I've heard of him," the former flatfoot commented, with a sneer. "There are a lot of players out there who'd like to mount your head on somebody's wall."

"I've met most of them," I replied.

"You must be made of iron," the sarcastic suspect continued. "You've survived shootings, explosions and at least five car crashes. "You've got to be the topic of conversation every time Pot Roast Sabastian sits down with his henchmen."

"I've learned a few things about you as well," I told him. "You were kicked off the force in Orlando for beating a suspect. More than a few shootings have been called into question. You've even been suspected of taking a bribe or two."

Fisher was clearly annoyed, but he understood the ramifications of blowing his top. "Those charges were bogus," he calmly contended. "As for the beating; that kid assaulted an eighty-year-old woman before pulling a knife on me. Get your story straight or stay out of my face!"

"Alright, that's enough!" the Sergeant asserted. "Mr. Fisher, I didn't have you hauled down here to take a trip down memory lane. So let's cut to the chase. We found some old newspapers in Connie Stewart's room. Your previous Orlando address was on one of them."

"So?" the suspect shrugged.

"When I questioned you last month, you denied ever having contact with the girl," the Sergeant reminded him.

"That was a mistake," Fisher conceded. "One day when the kid dropped by after school, she expressed an interest in becoming a cop. She was especially intrigued with this family of thieves who targeted banks and jewelry stores. She said she wanted to learn all she could about them. So I gave her a few old papers. I don't see the crime."

"Giving someone newspapers isn't a crime," Roy agreed. "However, lying to the Police can get you locked up. Your little memory lapse helped us convince a judge to sign off on a search warrant for your home."

"Search all you want," the intrepid person of interest dared. "You won't find anything that links me to Connie Stewart's disappearance."

"You're absolutely right," the Sergeant admitted, showing him a photocopy of a check for $3,000 that was made out to him and signed by Maxine Stewart. "But you might want to explain this."

Suddenly, the fearless loudmouth appeared at a loss for words. He looked down at the check and wiped his chin with his hand. Fisher may have been a madcap, but he was no dummy. If the cops suspected someone close to Connie of orchestrating her abduction, they could easily presume that a washed up detective who'd lost his pension had been paid to tie up a few loose ends. The jig was up and the only way to emerge from the flames without getting burned was to come clean about the $3,000 payment he'd received from Maxine Stewart.

"Alright," he said, taking off his hat and running his fingers through his thinning black hair. "Four months ago, Maxine hired me to look into the death of Ellen Mixon."

"Who's Ellen Mixon?" I asked.

"She was a patient at Tranquil Graces in Fort Meyers," Fisher explained. "It's a mental facility."

"What was Maxine's relationship to Ellen Mixon?" Roy inquired.

"She didn't say," the suspect replied.

"What did you find out?" I asked.

"Everything was pretty cut and dry," he told us. "Ellen Mixon slit her wrist with a piece of glass she found while on transport. An old friend with the Fort Meyers P.D. told me the autopsy report revealed no evidence of foul play."

"Was Maxine satisfied with your findings?" Roy asked.

"I think so," Fisher concluded. "I didn't feel right taking all the money, but she said the job was worth every penny. How do you get a grip on a broad like that?"

"I'm not sure," Roy responded. "But I intend to try."

"Can I go now?" Fisher asked. "Or do I need to call my lawyer?"

"That won't be necessary, Mr. Fisher," Roy told him. "You're free to go, but don't leave town. If Maxine Stewart doesn't corroborate your story, we'll be talking again."

Fisher put his hat back on and calmly headed out the door. Roy took a seat at the end of the table and sighed. The worried expression on his face was very familiar. I wanted him to tell me what was on his mind, but with the Sergeant, nothing was ever gained by prodding. So I just approached the situation from another angle.

"That old buzzard could juggle dynamite," I said, referring to Fisher.

"He probably has," Roy responded, staring at the wall.

"Do you think he had anything to do with the girl's disappearance?"

"He may have, but that's not our biggest concern right now. The child has been out there too long, Pete. If a predator does have her, he's bound to get bored and move on to another victim. If she hooked up with one of those crime families she idolizes, they've more than likely erased any trace of the decent young lady her parents raised. Time is running out, gumshoe."

Roy was right. Time was running out and he was no closer to finding her than he was two months earlier. I was also worried about Michael. After all the disappointments he'd already suffered, learning that his wife might have been involved in something criminal could have sent him over the edge. I was determined not to approach him until I knew what was going on with Maxine. The only way to uncover the truth was to find this complicated stepmother and give her an opportunity to explain why she'd been keeping secrets from her husband.

CHAPTER 16

After taking some time to gather his thoughts, Sergeant Van Eason signed out an unmarked unit and prepared to drive down to Fort Meyers. Since the trip would take several hours each way, we packed a couple of overnight bags and made arrangements to lodge at the home of Roy's favorite aunt. By daybreak, we were on our way.

It took a while to reach our destination, but a long and arduous excursion is easier to endure when passing the time with a trusted friend. Along the way, we witnessed some of the fury the recent blazes had wreaked upon homes, farms and wildlife. Thankfully, for the most part, the forest fires had subsided and officials were confident the worst was over.

Once Roy and I were settled, we wasted no time getting in touch with Tranquil Graces. Like the Sergeant, I wanted to learn the motive behind Maxine Stewart's interest in the death of Ellen Mixon. Van Eason placed a call to the facility administrator, Dr. Carson Henry, who met us in the ground floor storage room where the decedent's personal effects were packed away.

Dr. Henry had only supervised the institution for a short time, but he was the psychiatrist who treated Ellen Mixon.

Shattered lives and misdirected aggression were just a few of the elements that had composed this soft-spoken physician's universe for the past forty years. The bags beneath his somber green eyes revealed more about the toll the work had taken upon his life than any medical journal could ever convey. This seventy-year-old widower had sacrificed everything he treasured to defy the enemies of human contentment and guide the unenlightened to victory. Now, the burdens of time clung tightly to his weathered brow and his curly mane had turned to silver. A lifetime of catering to arrogant bureaucrats who worried more about the cost of care than the care of patients had drained his youthful idealism. In a few months, he'd be leaving that frustrating rat race behind him. Until then, there were hearts to mend and tempers to tame.

Surprisingly, the Tranquil Graces storage room wasn't the drab, dusty insect dominion portrayed in the movies. It was actually a well-kept enclosure with cardboard boxes neatly stacked on shelves containing the belongings of residents who'd either died or transferred to another facility.

Roy looked even more serious than usual in his department issue windbreaker. The .357 Magnum strapped to his waist added just the right touch. While I couldn't compete with the impression a uniformed police sergeant must've made, I thought my $150 leather basketball sneakers and the monogrammed jacket I'd purchased from the law enforcement academy in Gadsen County provided an air of authority that made people take notice. Though I'd never actually graduated from the school, enough hours of training had been completed for me to consider myself an honorary alumnus. At any rate, I was sure the doctor knew he was dealing with a couple of professionals.

Dr. Henry was a sad old man who seemed to carry the weight of the world on his shoulders. Throughout the span of his illustrious career, Ellen Mixon wasn't the only patient who'd taken her own life. The list of fatalities was long and vivid. Though he tried to view the losses as part of the job, a heart like his could never completely forget. He just wasn't that kind of man.

"We appreciate you taking the time to meet with us, Dr. Henry," Roy said, as we watched the benevolent administrator place a box containing Ellen Mixon's possessions on a table near the front exit. "I was advised that your responsibilities have doubled."

"That's because the Deputy Administrator, Dr. Barclay, is out of the country," Dr. Henry explained. "He's in the National Guard. They were sent to Afghanistan two weeks ago. Nonetheless, I must say I was surprised to receive your call. The death of Ellen Mixon was ruled a suicide."

"Doctor, let me assure you that we have no desire to make trouble for your facility," Roy said. "This is in connection with a missing persons case up in the Panhandle."

"A missing persons case," he repeated. "That's intriguing."

"Did anyone visit Ellen on a regular basis?" I asked.

"Her sister, Bertha, used to come see her every week," the Doctor replied. "But she hasn't been around in a few years."

"Why was she admitted to Tranquil Graces?" Roy asked.

Even though she was dead, Dr. Henry still considered Ellen his patient. So careful not to betray privilege, the conscientious psychiatrist endeavored to recall the details that were reported in the local media. "Well, I suppose the drug addiction would've landed her in here eventually," he said. "However, the loss of her child fifteen years ago seemed to be the defining tragedy that brought her down."

"Did the child die?" I inquired.

"No," he replied. "She was kidnapped."

His answer was shocking. We couldn't believe the irony.

"Did she have any idea who might have taken the child?" Roy asked.

"It was a trusted friend," he told us. "They'd been close for some time, but when Ellen began using drugs, the relationship changed."

"Did Ellen ever tell you the name of this friend?" I asked.

"In all the years I treated her, she wouldn't even reveal the woman's real name to me," Dr. Henry recalled. "Yet, when she spoke to reporters shortly after the abduction took place, she referred to the friend as "Pepper." According to Ellen, Pepper had gone to the Department of Children and Families, beseeching them to remove the child from her home. When her efforts failed, she took the baby one night and vanished. Since then, no one's heard from either of them. I'm sure the local authorities can give you Pepper's real name. That is, if Ellen ever revealed it to them."

"How long was Ellen here, Doctor?" Roy asked.

"Ten years," he said. "It's such a shame. I was sure she was on the road to recovery, but when Bertha stopped visiting her, Ellen took a turn for the worst." The Doctor looked at his watch. "Gentlemen, I'm sorry, but I have to go. Please let me know how things turn out."

"Certainly," Roy replied. "Thank you, Doctor."

When Roy lifted the lid off the box and began taking the items out, I was overwhelmed by the distressing chill that always invaded my mind at such a time. I couldn't get over how the life of an intriguing individual like Ellen Mixon had become little more than the relics of a downstairs storage room.

Ellen didn't have anything to leave the ones who mourned her passing. There was a Bible that once belonged to her grandfather. Several sketches of far-away places she'd only seen in magazines were neatly tucked between the pages of an old dictionary. She'd written letters to her daughter commemorating special occasions the two of them would never share. A disfigured doll in a tattered dress was wrapped in a towel. Post cards from a distant cousin describing his adventures at sea were sealed in a plastic bag. A letter from her sister, expressed the sorrow she felt at the loss of Ellen's child and the desire for vengeance that wouldn't go away. I felt like a pillager scavenging through the remnants of a grieving mother's distress. I had no right to unearth the pain Ellen carried every day. I could only imagine that if she were alive, she'd welcome the opportunity to reunite another parent with the child he loved so dearly. Perhaps then, all would be forgiven.

"There doesn't seem to be anything here that explains Maxine's interest in Ellen's death," Roy said.

"There has to be a reason why she would pay an investigator to look into the suicide of a woman who lived so far away," I said.

The Sergeant pulled out his blackberry and began checking his messages. "Well you keep looking," he told me, stepping over to the other side of the room. "I've got to call the station."

Convinced there had to be something hiding in plain sight, I began thumbing through the Bible. That's when I discovered what I'd been seeking. An old photograph of Ellen and her sister was the missing piece of this exhausting puzzle. An inscription pledging Bertha's never-ending love and devotion was written on the back of the picture. It was a beautiful gesture that would've remained unnoticed if the women with her arm around Ellen Mixon hadn't introduced herself to me as Maxine Stewart.

"Roy, take a look at this!" I exclaimed. "I found the connection."

The Sergeant examined the photo and looked at me. "This is incredible," he said. "Ellen Mixon was Maxine Stewart's sister."

"That's why she was so interested in the details of her death," I concluded. "When Maxine stopped visiting, Ellen committed suicide."

"But why did Maxine feel the need to keep all this quiet?" Roy wondered. "Could Ellen's past have been such a threat to her sister's new life?"

"It looks like the answer we found only leads to more questions."

"Questions that only Maxine can answer."

"We'd better get back home and find her."

There's something you need to know before we do that," my old friend said, touching my arm with an apprehensive look on his face.

"What's going on, Roy?" I asked.

"Awesome Anson English just made bail."

"Who has that kind of scratch?"

"He was sprung by a woman named Katrina Martin. She's an old acquaintance of yours."

"Katrina Martin? I've never heard the name."

"When you pulled the plug on her phony adoption enterprise, she was known as Uptown Patti Prather."

The Glass Fortress 73

Suddenly it all came back to me. Uptown Patti Prather was one of the slickest women I'd ever brought down. She was also believed to have fed Miles Trenton information about various corrupt officials. After one hand finished washing the other, Patti received a very light sentence and Trenton had the story of the year.

"I guess she's finally free," I said.

"Without a doubt," Roy responded. "I don't think it would take much to convince her to put up the money for a fellow criminal."

"But why would she bail English out?"

"Because someone she owes an enormous favor needs the big man's services."

"Trenton."

"Exactly...If I were a slimy creep looking for the right man to put a lid on the P.I. who'd been hired to clear the name of the man I'd framed, English would be the ideal candidate."

"Do you think he knows I'm on Michael's case?"

"He knows everything else."

I shook my head. "We've got to talk to Patti," I said.

"If we can get to her in time," Roy said.

"What do you mean?"

"Trenton is no amateur. I'm sure he's had you checked out. He's got to know it won't take you long to find out who sprung English. Uptown Patti Prather's days are numbered."

"We'd better hit the road," I said, as we headed out.

As usual, my old friend was absolutely right. Uptown Patti Prather was the only one who could link Trenton to the thugs he claimed to despise. Revealing that the demented newsman was the one who instructed her to post bail for Awesome Anson English could've caused irreparable damage to his squeaky clean image. That poor woman had become a liability Trenton could no longer afford.

CHAPTER 17

Sergeant Van Eason and I were on the road from noon till evening, hoping to make it back to town before Miles Trenton decided Katrina Martin, aka Uptown Patti Prather, had outlived her usefulness.

By the time we reached Panama City, Roy received a call from the Bunco Squad. Detective Ken Markus informed us that the officers assigned to bring Patti in found her residence abandoned and the front door wide open. According to a neighbor, she sped out of her driveway sometime around daybreak.

"This doesn't look good," Roy commented. "There could be a hundred reasons why a woman would take off so abruptly, but my money's on Trenton."

"Are Patti's parents still alive?" I asked.

"I don't know. They were pretty old when she was arrested. What are you getting at, Pete?"

"I remember how close they all seemed during the trial. It's hard to believe a couple of devoted parents like the Prathers wouldn't have left the family home to their only daughter."

Roy placed a call to the station and had one of his detectives run down an address for Lars and Nora Prather.

As I suspected, they had passed away, but their sturdy two-story brick home was still standing and well-maintained. The velvet green lawn had just awakened from its winter slumber. Lilies were in bloom and the replenished leaves of towering elms swayed proudly in the evening breeze. The seventy-six acre hideaway looked like the next best thing to paradise. Regrettably, like the bountiful haven that was lost so long ago, this serene oasis was about to be defiled by a venomous serpent bent on devouring anyone foolish enough to trust him.

Since the Prathers home was located on the outskirts of Burnadett, Roy was concerned that his officers might arrive too late to provide adequate backup. So he radioed the Highway

Patrol. With the extra forces watching our backs, we were sure we'd be able to get Patti out of the residence and take her into protective custody without incident. We couldn't have been more wrong.

The night was falling fast when Roy stopped the car on the shoulders of the blacktop road several hundred feet from Patti's driveway. The flashing strobe lights of two State Trooper units illuminated the yard as we stepped from the vehicle with our weapons drawn. The Sergeant took cover behind the front end of the car with an M-16 rifle at the ready while I positioned myself on the far side of the nearest patrol vehicle. That's when I spotted an injured State Patrol officer lying amongst the hedges along the front of the house.

A brown SUV was parked near the front door with the engine running. We had no way of knowing how many assailants were inside, nor what they'd done with the other Trooper. Moreover, if Patti was in the house, I was convinced her attackers weren't going to give her up without a fight.

"This is the Police!" Sergeant Van Eason shouted. "Lay down your weapons and come out with your hands up. We don't need any more bloodshed."

Suddenly, a masked gunman came charging out of the house with a semiautomatic handgun! The perp opened fire, shattering the windshield of the Sergeant's car as he made a break for the SUV. I fired a round into the fleeing hit man's side, taking him off his feet before he could reach the passenger side door.

A second shooter cautiously emerged from the house with his weapon trained on me. Roy was prepared to take him down, until a third accomplice revealed their trump card. He came out with a gun to the head of a female Trooper. Endeavoring to buy enough time for their injured comrade to take refuge inside the vehicle, the resourceful absconders held us in check with a fury of indiscriminate gunfire.

"You might as well give it up, cops!" one of them shouted, diving in through the rear window as the SUV sped away!

With my heart pounding and adrenaline pumping, I ran to the edge of the yard and took aim.

"Don't do it, Pete!" Roy admonished, reaching into his unit for the radio receiver. "You could be putting the life of the officer in danger. You'd better check on the other trooper while I call this in."

I stepped over the hedge and knelt down beside the brawny blond patrolman those masked assassins had left for dead. He was barely conscious and both eyes were swollen shut, but he didn't appear to have been shot. Gasping for breath and clinging to the buttons of his bloodstained shirt, this brave young officer attempted to speak. He was frightened and exhausted. We had to get him to a hospital. There wasn't a moment to waste.

Within minutes, Fire and Rescue descended upon the scene accompanied by five patrol units. As I watched the paramedics attend to the trooper, I could hear Sergeant Van Eason instructing his men.

"One officer has been taken hostage and another is critically injured," he told them. "I've already had an APB put out on the SUV and the Department of Law Enforcement has been notified. We'll need to get a forensics team out here, too. One of the punks was shot. There's a chance his DNA might be in the system. I want three of you to stay out here and secure the perimeter. The rest of you can come with me. We're going to search this place from top to bottom."

The officers stormed the house like soldiers on a mission. They went over the dwelling with a fine-toothed comb. Though they didn't find any other intruders, the discovery they did make was considerably more terrifying. The lifeless body of Uptown Patti Prather was lying across the bed in her upstairs guest room. The only witness who could say why Miles Trenton wanted Awesome Anson English out of jail was no longer a threat to anyone.

Upsetting the schemes of a man like Trenton was a dangerous move. When Michael Stewart made that mistake, he found himself wondering where he was going to spend the next few years of his retirement. For having the audacity to right the wrong that had been perpetrated against this innocent husband and father, I'd been sentenced to a daily routine of constantly looking over my shoulder.

Regardless of the cost, Trenton was willing to spend every dime at his disposal to keep his enemies at bay. In the case of Patti Prather, the self-consumed gangster could rest assured he'd gotten his money's worth.

CHAPTER 18

I'd spent most of the night at Police Headquarters, giving my statement and striving to remember any details that might help the boys in blue get a fix on the three hired guns that had kidnapped a state trooper. My head was pounding and my entire body ached. I was hungry and exhausted. Finding something to eat at 3:30 in the morning was a chore that could even baffle a detective of my vast experience and powers of deduction. Fortunately, my skills and eye for detail alerted me to the subtle clues that were hiding in plain sight. In layman's terms, I spotted a billboard for Lennie's All Night Cafe.

Lennie's was a quaint little place with a loyal clientele. The tables were clean and waitresses were friendly. Most evenings, the fearless roars of modern-day philosophers could be heard in every corner. However, when I sat down at a corner booth, the breakfast crowd had yet to arrive and a tiny television atop the counter was the only source of intelligent conversation in the immediate vicinity.

The waitress had already taken my order by the time Sergeant Roy Van Eason entered the place and joined me.

"You really need a vacation," I said, as I watched my old friend slowly take his seat. "A stressful job like yours can kill you."

"Now you tell me," he responded, placing a manila envelope on the table in front of me.

"What's this?"

"It's the file on Zeek Wilcox. He's believed to be the head of a bandit family operating in North Florida. We don't have much on him, but we now realize that he was the man Clark Milford saw in Vernon. I'm sure you remember me telling you that one of my officers discovered the story in Milford's diary. At the time, neither of us could've guessed she was talking about one of the most wanted men in the state." He noticed the perplexed expression on my face. "What is it, Pete?"

"I can't shake the feeling that I've met this man," I said, staring at the photo from a gas station surveillance camera. "This long-faced bearded character looks very familiar."

"I'm not surprised. You've ticked off half the criminal population of the Tri-states area."

"Does the press know about Wilcox?"

"I hope not. It would be to our advantage to keep a lid on this little family enterprise for a while."

"That reminds me. I'm almost certain someone at Michael's former place of employment is at the root of Connie's disappearance and Ann Kester is the common denominator. I think we should dig up everything we can about her death."

"I can have something for you this afternoon," he said.

I finally steered the conversation toward the question I didn't want to ask. "Any word on the troopers?" I inquired.

"The kid's name is Nick Palmer. He's been on the job for three years. His condition is serious, but the doctors believe he'll be alright."

"What about the hostage?"

"Shortly after you left the station, I received a call from the Department of Law Enforcement. The official word is that fifteen year veteran patrol officer, Lina Pembleton, was wounded and taken hostage while coming to the aid of a fellow trooper."

"I didn't see any indications of her being wounded."

"Neither did I, but the Crime Scene Unit determined that blood found in the house and on the lawn where the SUV was parked belonged to two different individuals. The thug you shot was the only one who got hit. If Pembleton is alive, she's more than likely in a world of hurt."

"Did the perp's blood match up with anyone in the system?"

"We won't know that until we hear from the lab."

I clutched my forehead and sighed. "Did you get a chance to speak with Maxine Stewart?" I asked.

"I called Michael," Roy told me. "But he said she'd taken a ride down to the beach in Panama City."

"I gather you didn't mention Ellen Mixon."

"I didn't want to confuse the issue with bits and pieces of a story I don't even understand. Hopefully, Maxine will come home and explain everything to her husband. She'd better be prepared to break this twisted scenario down to me as well."

When the waitress approached the table with our breakfast, I noticed a look of surprise on the Sergeant's face. "What's wrong?" I asked him.

"You ordered steak and eggs," he said.

"That's right. They've been your favorite for as long as I can remember."

"Am I really becoming so predictable in my old age?"

"Relax, gramps. You've still got a lot of good years ahead of you."

"Not if Miles Trenton has his way."

"I wonder where Trenton could've found that trio of butchers."

"With the kind of money that varmint is willing to spend; I wouldn't be surprised if they came to him."

"They're probably related," I said.

"How do you figure," Roy asked.

"I've been on the wrong end of a lot of shootouts and I've rarely seen thugs go out of their way to protect a wounded accomplice. Those three have a bond that's stronger than Miles Trenton's money."

"I'll have my detectives check with their informants. There might be a family of hit men who've recently come into a large sum of cash. We're also keeping an eye out for doctors with a history of aiding and abetting criminals in need of medical assistance."

As we began eating, an unexpected television report caught our attention.

"This just in from some of our crime beat sources," the anchorman said. "Authorities have reason to believe one of the bandit families that have plagued parts of Southern Florida are on the loose here in the Panhandle. You'll recall the bandit families are burglars and armed robbers who utilize the services of dastardly trained youngsters to perpetrate crimes against unsuspecting businesses. It is also believed that many of these mentors are the actual parents of the children. While details are sketchy at this time, we are aware that the Police have a name in connection with this particular gang. There are no mug shots to show you, but we do know a man named Zeek Wilcox is a person of interest. The fact that we are having so much trouble constructing the elements of this man's existence leads us to conclude that he functions under a cloud of many aliases. So until the entire picture comes into focus, we'll just have to keep digging. I'm Corbin Nettles for Channel 16 News. Now back to your regularly scheduled program."

Roy and I couldn't believe what we'd just heard. We sat there staring in amazement.

"How could this have happened?" I wondered aloud. "Could there be a mole on your staff?"

"I don't know, but I intend to find out," the Sergeant responded. "This throws a wrench in all the progress I thought we'd made. Making Zeek Wilcox aware that he's a suspect makes the almost impossible task of finding Connie Stewart even more insurmountable. This really stinks!"

The livid task force commander was absolutely right. If Michael Stewart's daughter was with the Wilcox family, there wasn't the slightest doubt that this crafty outlaw would be on his way across the country by sunset. We had to move fast.

CHAPTER 19

The media's betrayal of our best possible link to finding the missing girl was a jab to the bread basket that Roy and I didn't see coming. The pressure to find Connie Stewart was now more intense than ever. While the Sergeant fully appreciated the urgency of his present situation, he was equally concerned that someone in his division might have leaked extremely sensitive information to the press. The tightrope my inundated friend had been walking since this case began looked dangerously close to collapsing beneath his feet.

I wanted to hit the ground running and set out to find Zeek Wilcox, but Roy convinced me that I'd be no good to anyone if I didn't get some sleep. So I left Lennie's Cafe and headed home for a few hours of shuteye. Like so many times in the past, I lugubriously underestimated the depth of my exhaustion.

Though my clock-radio alarm was set to go off at noon, I didn't awaken until a few hours before midnight. Resting calmly in a state of mindless bliss, I strolled through the garden of surreal illusion, paying little credence to the world of murder and mayhem I seemed so helpless to escape.

I would've preferred to remain lost in the tranquil maze of my conflicted psyche, but I was snatched back to reality by a special report that described the shooting of a man suspected of illegally infiltrating the Police station. I didn't want to contemplate how much I'd missed during the past eight hours. Connie Stewart was still missing and Zeek Wilcox had every reason to be on a rocket to the moon. I felt anxious and disoriented. My only hope of reclaiming the squandered hours of a day gone by was to get cleaned up and head downtown. So after a quick shower and shave, I placed a call to Roy Van Eason's cell number. The Sergeant was clearly fatigued and rather cranky.

"Van Eason!" he grunted.

"Roy," I said. "It's me."

"Where are you, Masters?"

"I'm at home. I overslept. What's with you?"

He paused for a moment. "I'm sorry, Pete," he said. "This has really been a lousy day."

"I heard," I told him. "What's the deal with the perp who got shot?"

"He wasn't just any perp. His name was Craig Simon."

"I don't think I've ever heard of him."

"You knew him as "Needle-nose Mckenna.""

"The Chameleon?"

"That's right. The boys in White-Collar Crimes had been on his trail for the past three years. His usual MO was to assume an airtight identity and infiltrate a company long enough to learn something a rival business would be willing to fork over a fortune to know. After that, he'd sell what he'd collected to the highest bidder."

"No one expected him to finagle his way into a Police station," I commented.

"No," Roy agreed.

"So he was the one who leaked the name of your suspect to the press."

"Exactly. And that's not all. This kid fooled us and lingered under our noses for weeks. We look like idiots."

I'd known Roy long enough to realize something else was eating at him. "You might as well tell me the rest," I said.

"Simon was only twenty-four years old."

"I'm sorry, man."

"My boy, James, would've been twenty-one by now. I know the two lives were as different as night and day, but I can't help thinking about the wasted potential."

"James suffered a lapse in judgment," I assured the grieving father. "He was nothing like Simon."

"I know you're right," he said. "But getting into a car with a pack of stoned hoodlums didn't turn out any better than engaging the Police in a gun battle."

"Do you need to keep pursuing this case?"

"I don't have a choice, Pete. Michael's daughter is still out there and I can't watch another father bury his child."

"Well I'm heading out now," I told him. "I should be at the station within the hour."

"I'll see you then," Roy said as he hung up.

It had been a long time since Roy mentioned his late son. Though I would've done anything to take his pain away, the loss had left a wound that clever sentiments and good intentions wouldn't heal. I couldn't say I knew how it felt. Yet, with time and the loving shoulder of a caring friend, I prayed his burden would become a little lighter.

The temperature outside had plummeted about thirty degrees in the past few hours, so I put on the brown turtleneck sweater my Uncle Danny and Aunt Rose sent me from New York. I was almost out the door when the telephone rang.

Frustrated by my inability to control anything that had occurred since Mollie Fuller hired me, I was tempted to let it ring. On the other hand, I didn't want to miss something that might have led me to Connie. So I decided to pick up.

"Masters," I said.

"Mr. Masters," the nervous voice on the other end of the line muttered. "This is Maxine Stewart."

"Mrs. Stewart. You're a hard woman to find."

"I've had a lot to sort out."

"I can imagine. However, I'm in a tremendous hurry and I won't have time to talk to you tonight."

"You must be on the trail of Zeek Wilcox."

"That's right," I said. "I see you've been keeping up with news."

"I don't need some reporter to tell me anything about Zeek Wilcox," she responded. "We go way back."

That got my attention. "What are you trying to tell me, Mrs. Stewart?" I inquired.

"I'm telling you that I have everything you need to flush Zeek Wilcox out."

"Where are you now?"

"That's not important. Just meet me at the park in twenty minutes. You won't be sorry."

My best hope of cracking the case wide open abruptly hung up. "Mrs. Stewart!" I exclaimed. "Mrs. Stewart!"

I tended to worry when someone promised to present the answers to all my questions on a silver platter. In my experience, life just wasn't that simple. A river of suspicion came rushing through my mind as I pondered the possible motives of Maxine Stewart. For some reason that defied the boundaries of human comprehension, she might have been the one who had her stepdaughter kidnapped. What if she'd already murdered the girl? This unexpected telephone call could've been nothing more than an invitation to my own funeral. Every instinct I had told me to call the Police. This little drive to the park would either be the answer to a father's prayers, or the gravest mistake I'd ever make. At any rate, I had to know.

CHAPTER 20

The celestial beauty of resplendent constellations stippled across a boundless purple canvas above made it difficult to believe the world below could be so wrought with cruelty and violence. An unoccupied playground echoing the energy and laughter of innocent children seemed galaxies away from the abhorrent consequences that spawn from mortal man's inherent wicked tendencies. Surrounded by such exquisiteness, even a seasoned investigator might be inclined to overlook the cleverly concealed dangers of a windy spring night. However, the price of that mistake was higher than this P.I. was prepared to pay.

I backed my car into the driveway of a dilapidated house at the corner of Milton and Wynn. Though I was more than a hundred yards away from the place where I was supposed to meet Maxine, several vigilantly placed street lamps provided enough light for me to get a fairly decent look at the park.

A couple of cats were having the time of their lives scaling the jungle gym. The slide that protruded from the window of a giant plastic castle rocked back and forth as it endured the nettling of an unpredictable night wind. I could've sworn there was something lurking in the dark beyond the seesaws. I'd never felt more like a sitting duck. A mouse on the brink of snatching the cheese from a trap had better prospects for the future. I thought about taking off, but if Maxine Stewart had information that could lead me to Connie, I couldn't afford to pass it up. So I weighed the options and decided to make my move.

I opened the door and prepared to step out. It looked like my best bet was to find a strategic spot and take cover. I almost made it to the street, when a late model Cadillac entered the park. Since Maxine was the one who arranged this little get-together, it seemed reasonable to presume she was the driver of the solid black monstrosity. On the other hand, this case had taught me a thing or two about taking too much for granted.

I returned to my car and sat back down in the driver's seat. My plan was to observe the vehicle until I could get a look at the occupant. I should've been more concerned about the masked gunman who suddenly appeared at my passenger side window.

Though I couldn't see the stranger's face, a formal introduction wasn't necessary. He was definitely one of the shooters Roy and I confronted at Uptown Patti Prather's place.

The masked man motioned for me to roll down the window. "Take out that piece and gently lay it on the seat," he instructed.

"What is this?" I asked him, complying with his orders.

"Shut up!" the nervous gunman responded. "You'll find out soon enough. Now get out of the car and start walking."

He followed me across the street with that gun in my back. Despite his discomfort, it was evident that this punk was a pro. He stayed behind me the entire time and he never came close enough for me to disarm him.

As we entered the park and approached the Cadillac, a tall figure emerged from the back seat. Even without the hoards of adoring fans falling at his feet, there was no mistaking that arrogant strut. It was Miles Trenton in all his grandeur.

"Well what do we have here?" the conceited newsman asked with a repugnant smile.

"It's the incomparable Pete Masters. You have a nasty habit of sticking your nose into my business. But we're going to put an end to that tonight. It took a lot of planning to tail you. We had to use three cars. You really live up to your extraordinary reputation. Oh well, at least all the trouble we went to paid off."

"What do you want, Trenton?" I asked him.

"You like to get right down to business," he said. "That's a good trait. It's really too bad. A cat with your skills could've made a fortune working for me."

"I doubt that. Now get to the point."

"My beef with you is quite simple. I want you to drop Michael Stewart's case."

"Who?"

Trenton nodded to the masked goon behind me. Without warning, the ghastly thug planted his fist into my rib cage! I fell to my knees with an agonizing groan.

"I don't like it when people insult my intelligence, Masters," Trenton said, motioning for Awesome Anson English to step out of the car and join him. "You know exactly who I mean. Now I'm going to say this one time. You don't want to fool with me. Stewart is a demented animal who has been taking advantage of his own daughter. He deserves to hang."

"That's what you want everyone to think," I asserted, clutching my side. "Michael Stewart has never done anything to harm his daughter. He loves her. The only crime he committed was against your inflated ego. You had that letter planted in his home. Admit it, Trenton."

"Alright," the cavalier culprit agreed. "I planted the letter."

"Just like that?"

"Just like that. You see, Masters; I had a feeling you weren't going to cooperate. That's why I came prepared to leave your body floating in the Chattahoochee River. So I have no problem with you knowing that I'm responsible for Stewart's incriminating correspondence. While we're at it, I'll even cop to having Uptown Patti Prather taken out, too. After all, it's not like you'll be around to tell anyone." English handed his boss a .45 automatic. "It's a shame. You're such a smart guy."

I felt like a gazelle that had just wandered into the den of a man-eating lion. The look on Trenton's face was pure elation. The trigger-happy creep was prepared to end my life and I didn't seem to have any means by which to stop him. Yet, live or die, I wasn't about to go out on my knees. There was only one option. I had to rush him.

Hoping to throw Trenton off his game, I implored him to grant me one last request. "Wait!" I insisted, strategically shifting my body into attack mode. "I have something to say."

"Are you kidding me?" the bloodthirsty narcissist asked, as he slightly lowered the gun. "Your fate is sealed. Nobody turns me down."

I knew I wouldn't get another opportunity to take him down, so I took a deep breath and prepared to strike. I'd almost taken what was shaping up to be my last leap of faith when we were all startled by the unexpected blast of a .38 caliber revolver!

The round shattered the rear passenger side window of the Cadillac.

"Take cover!" English cried, reaching for his weapon.

Trenton fired three shots into the distant darkness. "Let's get out of here!" he ordered, heading for the car.

The masked rogue had to run past me to make his getaway, but before he could take a step, I scooped his legs out from under him and proceeded to extract a little payback with couple of jabs to the chin.

Despite the pounding I'd inflicted upon his face, my resilient adversary retained the cognizance to draw his weapon. I grabbed his wrists and gradually forced the barrel back. It looked like I was about to get the best of him, until the gun went off, winging me in the shoulder!

I tumbled backward and rolled across the grass, as the clandestine hoodlum beat a hasty retreat for the Cadillac. The shadowy figure dove in through the shattered back window, just as English put the pedal to the metal and sped out of there like a flaming bottle rocket!

Under more desirable circumstances, I would've made every effort to stop him, but with a bleeding shoulder and a pair of aching ribs, my heroic attributes were sorely lacking. The most immediate concern was getting out of that park before the happy hunter discovered I was still alive.

I stayed low and maneuvered toward the street. When I heard the roar of an approaching engine, I knew I was toast.

I turned around, shielding my eyes from the brightness of those piercing headlights, as I endeavored to see who was driving. Perceiving no other way out, I made a run for the giant igloo a few yards to my left. I'd almost taken cover when I heard the familiar voice of a woman.

"Mr. Masters!" she cried. "It's Maxine Stewart. I'm not going to hurt you. We've got to get out of here."

I hobbled toward the car, breathing like my heart was going to explode. Maxine opened the passenger side door and sat me down in the front seat.

"That shot in the dark came just in time," I said, as I watched her strap on the seat belt and pull away.

"I've always been pretty handy with a firearm," she responded. "I wasn't going to let that piece of trash take you out."

"Where are we going?"

"Some place safe."

"I need a doctor."

"Don't worry. I'll have a look at that shoulder. In the meantime, there are a few things you need to know."

With a pair of huge round shades tucked snuggly beneath the scarf around her head, Maxine personified the quintessential woman on the lamb. Those leather gloves and trench coat made me feel like we'd just missed the last plane out of Casablanca. Though I didn't know what this mysterious broad had in mind, I wasn't inclined to force the issue. After all, I was the one with the gunshot wound. For now, the only thing I could do was sit back and enjoy the ride.

CHAPTER 21

Maxine drove me to a little hideaway on the outskirts of town. She'd been crashing there for the past few days, contemplating the least destructive manner in which to ignite the powder keg of secrets that would change her husband's world forever.

I was tempted to call the rundown boarding shack a roach motel, but I didn't want offend the roaches. This crib was awful. There were cracks in the walls and the windows hadn't seen water since the last hurricane. The recliner in the corner reeked of beer and cheap perfume. Ashtrays overflowed with what I hoped were only tobacco remnants. That battered black carpet needed to be tested for radiation. I didn't even want to know the story behind the bloodstained towels scattered beneath the air conditioner. It was hardly a haven for the lost and downtrodden. Unfortunately, at the time, I couldn't afford to be picky.

My surreptitious rescuer sat me down on a bed that made more noise than a litter of puppies. Behind her tired and bovine expression, I could see the dread in her eyes. She knew the hard questions were coming. I just hoped she was willing to provide some honest answers.

"Take off your jacket and sweater," she said, as she took off her coat and headed for the bathroom. "There are a few clean towels I can rip up for bandages."

While she was gone I took a look around the room. There were enough greasy smudges on that rotary dial telephone to have been the smoking gun in at least forty unsolved homicides. Those drapes looked like they'd been used to polish heavy equipment. In fact the only thing in the place that didn't appear to have been there since the Great Depression was the plasma television set on the far wall. I thought about picking up the remote, but considering my surroundings, there more than likely wasn't anything on I needed to see.

When Maxine returned with the towels and a bed pan full of water, I noticed the brown bottle tucked under her arm.

"What's that?" I asked.

"This is peroxide," she said, twisting the cap off the bottle. "I can use it to clean the wound."

"You keep peroxide in your motel room?"

"You really aren't familiar with this part of town."

"There's a lot I don't know. I'm particularly baffled by the actions of my client's wife. She neglected to tell me that she'd hired Joe Fisher to look into the death of her sister."

Maxine didn't break a stride as she cleaned the wound and proceeded to bandage my shoulder. "I knew the day would come when I'd have to lay all my cards on the table," she said. "Ellen was more than just a strung out junkie who died too young. She was also the victim of the most horrific crime a mother can experience."

"The abduction of her child."

"I see why you come so highly recommended. You're absolutely right. Ellen was devastated. I didn't even know about the drug problem. I would've been happy to take the girl until she could get clean."

"Where were you when it all went down?"

"I was working at a hospital in North Carolina. By the time I heard about the kidnapping and returned home, my sister was a wreck."

"Dr. Henry said the child was taken by a friend Ellen called Pepper."

Maxine finished patching my shoulder up and sat down beside me. Her stolid demeanor turned to rage before my very eyes. "That woman was no friend!" she snarled. "They went to high school together. Ellen trusted that scheming witch with her life. I couldn't believe she'd done something so vile. I spent years tracking her down."

"Did you ever find her?"

"Oh yes."

"Where was she?"

"Living with my husband."

Despite the crudeness of her answer, I presumed she was talking about someone she was married to before she met Michael. "Michael never mentioned you'd been divorced." I said.

"I haven't," she responded.

I slowly rose to my feet suspecting the worst, but I didn't want to jump to conclusions. "What are you telling me, Maxine?" I inquired.

"I'm telling you that Michael's first wife, Delta, was the woman who kidnapped my sister's baby."

I was astounded. I paced the floor for a moment. That's when an even more upsetting thought popped into my head. "That would make Connie Ellen's stolen child," I concluded.

"That's right," she confirmed.

"Didn't Delta recognize you as her old friend's sister?"

"I'd already graduated by the time they got to high school. Besides, I have changed quite a bit over the years."

"No wonder you and Connie shared such a bond. You're her aunt."

"We hit it off right from the start. She always said I was the only one who really understood her. I wish I could have told her the truth."

"Why didn't you?"

"Because my first priority was to get close to Delta."

"I don't understand."

"Getting to know her habits and making her comfortable with me would've made it easier for me to kill her."

"So you followed her here to seek vengeance for what she did to Ellen. It looks like your plans were spoiled by your intended victim's natural demise." I said. I saw her look away. "Or was it natural?"

"No," she admitted. "I killed her."

"How?"

"I became her girlfriend. We talked about our fears, regrets and plans for the future. She soon began to trust me like a sister. Some nights we'd stay up watching old movies. We even spent time volunteering for community activities. One day I asked her to let me do her hair. That was the beginning of the end for the baby snatcher."

"What did you do?"

"Have you ever heard of Tetrachloroethane, Masters?"

"I've heard the name. Isn't it some kind of dry cleaning agent?"

"That's one of its uses. It's also used in the manufacturing of silk, leather and pearls when employed for the right purpose."

"And what would be the wrong purpose?"

"Inducing the death of an evil jezebel and enjoying every minute of her suffering."

I was amazed at how calmly she answered my question. Right or wrong, this woman felt justified. "How did you pull it off?" I asked.

"It wasn't difficult," she responded. "I kept the Tetrachloroethane in a spray bottle and applied it every time I styled her hair. The symptoms were hardly noticeable at first. She complained of eye, nose and throat irritation. After that, the drowsiness and vomiting set in. I rarely left her bedside. Michael even suspected alcoholism. The dermatitis should've been the last nail in my coffin, but no one suggested foul play. When she finally died, I had all my affairs in order. I was going to be on the next plane out of the country."

"What changed your mind?"

"There was no autopsy."

"What?"

"I'm telling you the truth. The official cause of death was kidney failure. No one asked any questions. So I just kept my mouth shut and played my part as the grieving best friend."

"Weren't you taking a big chance by sticking around and marrying the victim's widower?"

Maxine stood up and walked to the window. Cautiously separating the drapes, she peered out into the night. "I never meant to fall in love with Michael," she said. "The pain and emptiness in our hearts was just too much for either of us to bear alone. My husband is such a good man, Masters. After Delta's death, he wanted to tell Connie she was adopted, but he didn't know how she would be affected. He loves that child with all his heart."

"How does Zeek Wilcox play into all of this?"

"Zeek is Ellen's ex-husband. He's also Connie's biological father."

That was the biggest bombshell I'd stumbled across since the case began. I ran my fingers through my hair and shook my head. "Are you kidding?" I asked.

"No," she replied, opening the envelope and showing me the very photo of the dastardly dad I'd seen on the news.

"Why didn't he take Connie when your sister was on drugs?"

"He couldn't. The punk was in prison. He did five years for grand theft-auto. Besides, you already know how he's ruined the lives of his other children. Can you imagine what he would've done to Connie if he'd had the chance to raise her from infancy? Zeek Wilcox is as low as they come."

"How did Connie find out about him?"

"I don't know. I'm sure she learned all she could on the web, but someone had to tell her the rest."

"You've known Connie long enough to know how she feels about stealing. Do you think she would take part in the family business?"

"That's hard to say. In spite of how I felt about Delta, she and Michael did a fine job rearing the child. On the other hand, little girls really love their daddies. There's no telling what she'd be willing to do to please her newfound Pop."

Maxine put her coat back on and headed for the door.

"Where are you going?" I asked.

"I've got a plane to catch," she said, tossing the envelope down on the bed. "You've got everything you need to put Zeek Wilcox away for good."

"What about Michael?"

"I left him a long letter explaining my role in Delta's death. I don't expect him to forgive me, but he deserves to know the truth. When you see him, please tell him I'm sorry."

"You can tell him yourself," I said, reaching for the telephone. "You're going back to town and turn yourself in."

Had I been thinking clearly, I wouldn't have turned my back on an armed murderess who had just confessed to killing her husband's first wife. The fact that she didn't bother to argue should've sent up a flare. Nevertheless, I carelessly dialed 911 and provided the perfect opening for Maxine to cross my lights.

"I'm sorry, Masters," she said, as she retrieved the revolver from her coat pocket and read me the final chapter of the desperate woman's handbook.

Looking on the bright side, I had to admit that single blow to the back of the head did make me forget the pain in my shoulder. When I hit the floor, everything in the room became as dark as that revolting carpet.

So there I was, stranded in the seediest part of town with no weapon and no vehicle. I'd been ambushed, beaten and shot. Without medical attention, I stood a good chance of bleeding to death. I would have considered the piercing wails of distant sirens to be an encouraging sign if the only person who knew where I was hadn't just confessed to premeditated murder. I desperately needed to think about going into another line of work.

CHAPTER 22

Throughout the span of my fifteen-year career, the faces of many victims had been splattered upon the sills of my memory. I'd held the hand of a sobbing bride who'd just learned her conniving groom cleaned out her bank account and skipped town with the matron of honor. The hollow gaze of a terrified father dreading to inform his children of their mother's suicide had never faded. Tears of betrayal streaming down the cheeks of a violated little girl mourning the trust and innocence she would never possess again gave me nightmares that tormented my mind for months. Yet, I couldn't recall anything more disturbing than a grieving parent struggling to understand how a senseless tragedy could have claimed the life of his only son.

I had seen that look on the face of my friend, Roy Van Eason, many times. The fear of losing someone else he loved had the Sergeant on edge. Though I couldn't blame him for being outraged, the scolding would've been slightly more bearable if he'd arrived a few minutes after my morphine shot.

When Roy entered the Emergency Room of Mount Sinai Memorial Hospital lugging a bulging duffel bag, he looked like a man who'd just found out how much of the minimum payment is attributed to the actual credit card bill. This wasn't going to be fun.

"What did you think you were doing?" the Sergeant asked. "You could've been killed!"

"Nice to see you, too, old friend," I grunted, pressing the button to raise the head of my bed.

"Don't try to be funny, Gumshoe. I'm not in the mood."

"I know, Roy. I'm sorry. I was on my way to the station when Maxine called. She claimed to have information about Zeek Wilcox. I couldn't ignore an opportunity to get a lead on Connie."

He dropped the duffel bag and sat down on the bed. "I'm the one who should be sorry," he said. "It feels like somebody cut a piece of my heart out, Pete. The house is so empty without him."

"James was a fine young man."

"He sure was."

"Is there anything I can do?"

He looked at me with a partial smile. "You can stop running off on these solo suicide missions!" he insisted.

"You got it, Sarge," I promised.

Roy reached into the bag for an envelope. "We found this on the bed beside your barely conscious body," he said. "It's a collection of photographs. Most of them depict Zeek Wilcox going about his daily routine. As you might have guessed, the fagin is no boy scout."

The Sergeant was absolutely right. Zeek Wilcox had been caught on tape committing more than ten robberies. It was enough evidence to put him away for a very long time. Nonetheless, I was more focused on the picture of Wilcox standing in front of a picnic table with his mother and eleven-year-old son.

"What do you see?" Roy asked.

"It can't be the same," I muttered.

"What are you talking about, man?"

"Look at the brooch the lady is wearing," I said, showing him the picture.

"It looks like a nice piece of jewelry. I wouldn't mind getting my hands on a rock like that."

"You won't have to go far."

"Why do you say that?"

"Because I saw it in Tim Herbert's office."

"It belongs to him?"

"No, Jodie Parker was wearing it in a photograph. It would take a lot of blows to the head to make him give her anything. But I would like to know how an expensive brooch that belonged to the mother of Zeek Wilcox ended up with a woman on a mail room salary."

I forced myself up and placed my feet on the floor.

"What are you doing?" Roy asked.

"I've got to get dressed," I told him. "Do you know where they put my clothes?"

"We had to keep your sweater and windbreaker for evidence," he said. "But there's a department issue hooded sweater and a pair of trousers in the bag. I put your gun in there, too. If I have to recover that piece one more time, I'm collecting a finder's fee."

"Thanks, old friend," I said, gathering the clothes. "However, I wouldn't count on making a case against Maxine Stewart. She's headed out of the country."

"The car she was driving was a rental. The GPS led us to a ramshackle old dance studio near the state line."

"Then you have her."

"No, the car was abandoned. She'd obviously made arrangements to leave in another vehicle."

"That lady is too much. What about my car?"

"I parked it in your driveway after Forensics looked it over."

"You always look out for me, Roy."

After I retreated into the bathroom to splash a little water on my face and change, Roy's cell phone rang. I could hear him responding to the person on the other end of the line. The conversation didn't sound like good news.

"What?" the Sergeant inquired. "Well when did it happen? Where is she now?…Alright, thanks."

"What's going on, Roy?" I asked, returning to the room fully dressed.

"At least we don't have to worry about finding Jodie Parker."

"What happened?"

"She's here."

"In this hospital?"

"A neighbor found her beaten half to death on the kitchen floor. They've got her upstairs in Intensive Care."

"Well let's go," I said, as we headed out.

When we reached the elevator, I attempted to press the button, but my shoulder didn't want to cooperate. "Woe!" I exclaimed, clutching my forearm.

"You should be in bed," Roy insisted. "When that doctor checked on you earlier, he said he wanted to keep you for at least twenty-four hours."

"I'm fine, flatfoot. Besides, we've got to talk to Jodie Parker."

The doors parted and the two of us stepped inside. This time I let Roy handle the controls. On the way up, it occurred to me that the Sergeant hadn't brought up my arch enemy.

"What's the deal with Miles Trenton?" I asked.

"You won't have to worry about Mr. Trenton for a long time."

"Why not?"

"Maxine recorded your meeting in the park on her camera phone and sent it to me. Trenton and his cronies are being picked up as we speak."

"His unscripted performance should be enough to get the charges against Michael Stewart dropped."

"The ball is already rolling."

"Michael has really gone through a lot."

"You're right about that. I can't say I know how he feels, but I'm quite familiar with the thoughts that run through your mind when something happens to your child. I just hope Michael will be able to keep his head on straight."

When we reached the fourteenth floor, Roy caught sight of a doctor heading around the corner. He still had the file on Zeek Wilcox. "I'm going to have a word with that doctor," he said.

"Leave the file with me," I requested.

He handed me the folder and darted down the corridor.

No one was manning the nurse's station, so I placed the family portrait on the desk to examine it one more time. I didn't want to get bogged down on what might have been an insignificant detail, but I was certain this wasn't the first time I'd laid eyes upon the deceitful mug of Zeek Wilcox.

Despite what the renegade father had become, I was touched by the endearing portrayal of a loving family. The heavy-set lady in the sepia brown dress amorously clutched the shoulder of the dapper young boy standing in front of her. Even Wilcox appeared to embody the wholesome criterion that shaped his mother's dreams as he rested his hand at the base of her curly sable mane.

It was a precious moment captured in time forever. The only flaw maligning this masterpiece of treasured serenity was the ubiquitous brooch that had yet to be explained.

When Roy returned, he stood at the entrance of IC Unit 12 and beckoned for me to approach. His expression didn't foster a lot of hope.

"What's wrong?" I asked.

"Jodie Parker is in there," he said. "The doctor said she sustained several blows to the head. So she's likely to fade in and out of consciousness. He's allowing us five minutes to see what she can tell us. I promised not to upset her. If reliving the experience becomes too much for her, the conversation is over. We don't want to risk doing anything that might worsen her condition."

"I understand."

As Roy and I entered the room, I tried to imagine what kind of animal could have inflicted such brutality upon an unsuspecting woman. Jodie looked like she'd been hit by a train. Every moan and groan sent chills up my spine. The disoriented victim's head was bandaged and her vital signs were being monitored by machines that even a veteran patient like me didn't recognize. Her face was sullied with cuts and bruises. Three broken ribs made the simple act of breathing a laborious challenge. I hated the thought of burdening her with intrusive questions concerning the person she loved more than anyone else on earth. Had there been another way to learn what I needed to know, I wouldn't have hesitated. Yet, as it stood, the only bridge between me and the truth was lying helpless in that hospital bed.

"Ms. Parker," Roy whispered, cautiously approaching Jodie. "It's Sergeant Van Eason and Pete Masters."

"Van Eason," she repeated, breathing heavily. "You're the cop who's looking for Michael's daughter."

"That's right," the Sergeant confirmed, taking the file from me and showing her the picture of the Wilcox Family. "We understand how difficult this must be for you, so we'll be brief. The brooch in this photograph is the same one you wore to a charity banquet a few weeks before Ann Kester died. Can you tell us how it came into your possession?"

"The brooch belonged to Ann," she said. "Her boyfriend gave it to her. She didn't want anything that reminded her of him."

Without saying another word, Jodie rolled over and closed her eyes.

Roy closed the file and walked back over to me. "Well she didn't tell us much, but at least we know where she got the brooch," he said.

"This mystery boyfriend seems to be the key to everything," I determined. "I wish I could talk to someone who met this guy before Ann Kester killed herself."

When Jodie heard Ann's name, she raised her head. "Barbiturates," she muttered.

"What was that, Ms. Parker," Roy asked.

"Ann took an overdose of barbiturates," she said. "That's how she killed herself."

As Jodie turned away and drifted off to sleep, I clutched my forehead. I couldn't believe what I'd just heard.

Roy noticed my reaction. "What is it, Pete?" he inquired.

"Is that true?"

"What?"

"Did Ann Kester use barbiturates to take her own life?"

"That's right. What's going on in that head of yours?"

"I couldn't see the resemblance because of the beard. If we hadn't been distracted by the woman with the baby carriage, I would've caught his slip immediately."

"Slip!" Roy exclaimed. "What are you talking about, man?"

"Roy, we're going to need a warrant."

"Would you mind letting me in on the big secret?"

"I'll tell you on the way," I assured him as we headed out.

Finally, everything was beginning to make sense. Without realizing it, Jodie Parker had cracked the case.

After a grueling half-hour of trying to convince the doctors that I would return to the hospital if I felt the need, I was allowed to sign some papers and leave. Afterward, Roy and I headed for the courthouse. As far as we knew, the man we wanted was still at large and he had no reason to wait around for a visit from us.

CHAPTER 23

Sergeant Van Eason and I kicked in the door of Chuck Wheeler's apartment a few minutes past noon. I was convinced the young janitor had severely beaten Jodie Parker, so we entered the residence with our weapons drawn. Considering the violence our suspect was capable of, we had to be ready for anything. I wouldn't have been surprised to find the seasoned con artist waiting to mow us down with an arsenal of automatic rifles, but to our dismay, he'd vacated the premises. However, nothing could've prepared me for what we did find.

Michael Stewart was lurking around the kid's room, rummaging through what personal belongings he'd left behind. The Sergeant and I were shocked.

"Don't shoot!" Michael pleaded. "I'm unarmed."

"What are you doing here, Michael?" Van Eason demanded.

"I received a call from Connie's friend, Karen," the frightened intruder explained. "She was at some convenience store near the Panama City cutoff. Chuck Wheeler picked her up from school and said he had an idea where Connie might have gone. By the time she realized he wasn't on the level, the punk started getting crazy. He didn't know she had her cell phone."

"Why didn't you call me?" Roy asked.

"No offense, Sergeant," Michael responded. "But the last attempt at procuring justice didn't exactly result in a happy ending."

"How did you get in here?" I asked Michael.

"When I told Karen's mother what happened, she gave me Wheeler's address," he explained. "Getting into the apartment required a skill I'd rather keep to myself."

"Good call," the Sergeant commented.

"What are you two doing here?" Michael inquired. "And why did you kick the door in?"

Roy looked at me and sighed. He was about to reveal what we'd discovered in the past twenty-four hours, but before he could utter a word, his cell phone rang. "I've got to take this," he said, as he went into the bathroom.

"Well I guess it's up to you, Masters," Michael concluded. "Dump another load of misery into my lap. Although I doubt anything you have to say can make me feel worse than I do right now."

"I gather you read Maxine's letter."

"Can you believe this? Just when I thought I'd scraped the very bottom, my wife confesses to murder. Even the first marriage was built on a foundation of lies."

"Did she tell you about Zeek Wilcox?"

"Oh yes. I spent all those years wondering how I was going to tell Connie the truth about her paternity. It never occurred to me that Delta wasn't her mother. Ah, this is such a huge mess."

"It's bigger than you think."

"What now?"

I sat down on the bed and looked up at this broken man. I didn't want to tell him the rest, but too much deceit had already darkened his doorstep.

"Karen felt guilty about an argument she had with Connie concerning the time she'd been spending with Chuck Wheeler," I told him. "She thought there was something going on between them."

"She told me," he responded. "But that's just teenage silliness. "I couldn't hold it against the child."

"There wasn't anything romantic between Wheeler and your daughter."

"How can you be so sure?"

"Because Wheeler is Connie's brother."

Michael ran his fingers through his hair and leaned against the wall. "The drama never ends," he said. "How did you find out?"

"When I saw Zeek Wilcox on the news, he had a beard. Even though his son is the spitting image of him, I didn't immediately make the connection. I wasn't able to see the resemblance until Sergeant Van Eason gave me a photo of Wilcox with his family. Then I remembered what the kid said about Ann Kester."

"Ann? What does she have to do with any of this?"

"You mentioned that Ann turned to you after breaking up with her boyfriend."

"That's right."

"Well no one seemed to know the identity of this mystery lover."

"What are you getting at, Masters?"

"Did you know Ann had fibromyalgia?"

"No," he said, taking a few steps toward me. "She never said a word."

"I'm not surprised," I commented. "In fact, the only one she told was her boss, Mollie."

"I still don't see your point."

"When I spoke to Chuck Wheeler about Ann's death, he said he'd never met her. He could only repeat what he'd heard other people say about the incident. That's what gave him away."

"Gave him away? What do you mean, man?"

"A split-second after he answered my question, we were distracted by a woman with a baby carriage who was almost struck by an oncoming motorcycle. If she hadn't appeared, I would've noticed that Wheeler said Ann died from an overdose of pregabalin."

"What's pregabalin?"

"It's a medication for fibromyalgia."

Michael sat down on the bed beside me. "He wouldn't have known what was in her medicine cabinet unless they were close," he concluded.

"Exactly," I agreed. "Chuck Wheeler was the mystery boyfriend."

"I can't believe this."

"I would've missed it if Jodie Parker hadn't told us that Ann overdosed on barbiturates."

"But why did she keep the relationship a secret?"

"I believe it was because she was ashamed of being taken in by a smooth-talking swindler who inevitably revealed his true colors."

"Could this kid really be so devious?"

"He's that devious and more."

"I don't understand."

"Jodie Parker is in the hospital."

"What happened?"

"I think she discovered the connection between Ann's brooch and the Wilcox Family."

"Could he be vicious enough to strike a woman Jodie's age?"

"I believe so. That's why we have to bring Connie and Karen home before it's too late."

I could see the tears in the grieving father's eyes as he endeavored to look away. "This is a nightmare," he said.

"I hate the way this makes you feel, but I had to tell you the truth," I said.

"I just don't know how this could've happened. A year ago, I was a widower with a troubled teenage daughter. Now, I don't know what I am."

"You're the same loving father you were then."

"Haven't you heard? I'm not her father."

"You are in every way that matters."

Michael stood up and paced the floor as he stroked the back of his neck. "I know I shouldn't feel this way," he said. "I've seen so many people who would give anything to trade places with me. I should be thankful. It just seems like I've devoted my very being to a way of life that has meant practically nothing. Don't get me wrong. I don't claim to be a saint, but I was loyal to my family. I tried to give Connie everything she needed to become a happy and productive adult. Even though we didn't share the same DNA, I loved that child with all my heart. To me, that was all that mattered."

"It's still all that matters," I insisted.

"I don't know what to do, Masters. I'm afraid I'm going to lose my little girl. When I think of her getting shot in some holdup, I could just die. She could be gone before I ever get the chance to say how much I love her. Her final moments won't be of shared memories and timeless laughter. She'll only remember the parents who lied to her for sixteen years."

"I wish I could say something that might put all of this into perspective for you, Michael. But the sad truth is that I don't understand it myself. We just have to believe that being a decent, loving man is its own reward. If you'd taken a different course, you never would've turned Delta's head. And despite what you've recently learned, it was your marriage to her that brought Connie into your life. The lengths Mollie is willing to go to protect you says more about your character than I could ever put into words. Ann would never have willingly shared her feelings with a man who didn't have an honest heart. The breakup with Chuck Wheeler proved that. Don't let this darkness blind you to the light of who you really are. Continue to be a friend to those who feel unworthy of friendship. Comfort the lonely and cherish every minute you had with Connie. I can't tell you what tomorrow will bring, but I do know your love for that child is not in vain."

An awkward silence clouded the room like an eerie fog. I couldn't distinguish whether Michael was in a state of deep meditation, or simply battling with the inclination to flip me off. I was tempted to inquire, but when Sergeant Van Eason came storming from the bathroom, a more pressing matter became the focus of our attention.

"Where's the fire, Roy?" I asked.

The officer held his blackberry up and showed us a picture of an old man in a wheelchair.

"Who is that?" Michael asked.

"It's Chuck Wheeler," Roy replied. "He died three years ago in a Homestead nursing home."

"So the man we know as Chuck Wheeler is an impostor," Michael said.

"That makes sense, considering the crimes he and his father have committed," I said.

"I don't know how much of this room Michael has contaminated," Roy said, walking over to the telephone to check Wheeler's messages. "But I want the Crime Scene Unit to go over every speck of dust. I took a look in the medicine cabinet. The kid's razor and toothbrush are still here. So he may not be gone for good. I'll station a unit across the street in case he comes back."

The first message was from Zeek Wilcox. "It's your dad, kid," he said. "I'm still waiting for that package. Bring it to me now. We don't have much time."

"That didn't tell us much," Roy commented.

"I wonder what kind of package Wilcox is expecting," Michael said.

"He's probably talking about Karen," I said. "She and Connie spent a lot of time with his son. I doubt he wants to see her pointing at him from the witness box."

Despite our increasing disillusionment, the second message provided a considerable air of possibility.

"Hi, Chucky," the voice of a jaunty young woman said. "It's Brandi. You promised to call me when you left St. Augustine, but I haven't heard from you. If you're in the mood for a walk down memory lane, I'm at the Peddler's Lodge Inn. It's the one I was staying at when we met. You know the place. See ya later, stud."

"Wheeler gets around," Michael concluded. "Now all we have to do is drive to the Peddler's Lodge Inn and ask the right questions."

"We're not going anywhere," I asserted. "The Sergeant and I will go to the Inn."

"You've got two problems," Roy contended. "There are six Peddler's Lodge Inns in town. It could take days to cover them all and time is not on our side."

"Can't you assign a few extra officers to show Wheeler's picture around?" I suggested.

"That's the second problem," the exhausted task force commander responded. "That call I received was from the Chief of Detectives. The Commissioner has called for an inquiry into the events that stemmed from the Department's affiliation with Miles Trenton. My team and I will be out of action for at least two weeks."

"I'll just have to pound the pavement on my own," I said.

"Why won't you guys let me help?" Michael asked.

"No," "Roy insisted. "You're too emotionally involved. The best thing for you to do is keep Mollie informed. She's going to need all the friends she has before this is over."

"By the way, Roy," I said. "Did you get a hit on Wheeler's true identity?"

"The photograph I showed you had the names of Zeek Wilcox and his Mother, Rita, written on the back," he explained. "But the boy was merely referred to as Zeek's son. We weren't able to learn much about him, but we did discover that Rita's prints are in the system."

"She has a record?" I inquired.

"No, but she was employed by the Department of Juvenile Justice for fourteen years," the Sergeant replied. "She filed a report with the Tampa Police when her grandson was seventeen. He'd run away."

"That's probably when he decided to join the family business," I concluded. ""What's his real name?"

"Paul Thomas Wilcox," Roy said with a suspecting squint. "Listen to me, Pete. This information doesn't give you the green light to play cowboy. If you find Wilcox or his son, call for backup. Is that clear?"

"I promise, Sarge," I replied.

Roy walked over to Michael and put his hand on the mortified father's shoulder. "You're going to get through this," he told him.

"Thanks, Roy," he responded.

"Don't forget what I said, Pete," the Sergeant admonished, as he headed out.

As I stood there observing the terrified expression on Michael's face, I was reminded of the time when a tired-looking, disheveled old man knocked on my door and asked for something to eat. I made him a sandwich and gave him fifty bucks. A week later, he was shot by a bookie looking to collect on a gambling debt.

I remembered thinking how much better I would've felt if I had known about the monkey on his back. At the very least, I could've steered him in the right direction.

Now, Michael was the old man at my door and this time I'd done everything in my power to help him. It's funny. I still didn't feel any better.

CHAPTER 24

From a distance, the Peddler's Lodge Inn looked like a stack of toy blocks some kid left out in the rain. The drab fifteen story eyesore was nestled amid twenty acres of the most beautiful scenery in Northwest Florida.

Unlike many of the hotels and tourist attractions along the Gulf Coast, the Inn seldom catered to spring breakers. The majority of its clientele consisted of older vacationers who didn't want to be thought of as snowbirds. Those venerable party animals enjoyed the same amenities as their junior counterparts. At any time during the day, the young at heart could be found frolicking in the pool while others partook of refreshments beneath the shade of a turquoise awning. The place was a senior citizen's paradise. It seemed strange that a girl Brandi's age would choose to stay there. On the other hand, I had no reason to complain. A young woman strolling through the halls of the Peddler's Lodge Inn had to stick out like a sore thumb. That tidbit of circumstantial frivolity was going to make my job a lot easier.

I approached the entrance intensely focused on finding Brandi. That's probably why I wasn't overly concerned about the ghastly expressions on the faces of some of the guests. I presumed they were more than likely astounded to see someone clad in a corduroy jacket on a sunny spring morning. For a group of fun-loving New Englanders who were used to braving sub-freezing temperatures, a frigid breeze in 65 degree weather provided a perfect excuse to light the fuse of eternal youth and explode all over anyone who got in their way. However, to me, it was just cold.

I wasn't the only southerner who felt the chill of an extended winter. The wavy-haired young man in charge of maintaining the pool was wearing an East Burnadett High School sweater and blue jeans. The scraggy grouser looked like he was going to freeze as he took a drink from his thermos.

His name was Tyler Jacobs. Though he was only in his mid twenties, the consummate complainer's discontent dated all the way back to the Civil War. Nothing seemed to satisfy this aimless loner. In his estimation, the world was a crowded station where droves of losers waited anxiously to board a speeding train to nowhere. I could tell by the unrepentant pessimist's deliberate scowl that a conversation with him would take me to a bleak and hollow place. Nevertheless, I needed to hear what he had to say. Besides, a man who found fault with everything and everyone wasn't going to miss an opportunity to shower an intrepid seductress with the merciless condemnation she so vehemently deserved.

To say the least, young Mr. Jacobs wasn't taken with the festive dispositions of our neighbors from the north. He seemed even less impressed with me.

"Excuse me," I said as I approached him with a manila envelope in my hand. "My name is Masters. I'm a private investigator."

"Good for you," he responded. "What do you want?"

"I'd like to ask you a few questions."

"Time is money, big man."

I reached into my pocket for a fifty-dollar bill. "Will this buy me a few minutes?" I asked.

"It couldn't hurt," he said, reaching for the money.

I showed him the picture of Paul Wilcox that Mollie Fuller had pulled from her personnel files and faxed to Sergeant Van Eason. "Have you seen this man?" I inquired.

"I've seen him. The guy's a real jerk."

"Why do say that?"

"Are you kidding? You'd have to be blind to think that girl was legal."

"What girl?"

"The big chick he checked in with yesterday."

I also had a picture of Karen. "Is this the girl?" I asked.

"That's her," he grimaced after taking another sip from his thermos. "I almost feel sorry for her."

"Why?"

"Because he's two-timing the kid. I saw him with that Brandi broad when I came back to get something from my locker last night."

"Do you know Brandi?"

"I know the type."

"The type?"

"You know what I mean. She's one of those painted prom queens who thinks a wink and a smile entitles her to anything she wants."

"Can you tell me her room number?"

Jacobs raised his brow and tilted his head forward. I didn't have to wonder what was on his mind. Another twenty turned out to be the remedy for his chiropractic discomfort.

"She's in Room 506," he told me. "But be careful. I saw a couple of baboons lurking in the hallway. I didn't know what was going on and I didn't ask any questions."

"Thanks, kid," I said as I headed inside.

It took a little fast-talking, but I finally convinced the manager that his part in the rescue of an abducted teenage girl could add up to a considerable amount of untapped revenue once the media got wind of the story. So after making certain the valiant concierge was safely tucked away in his office, I used the key he gave me to unlock Brandi's door.

I entered 506 with my weapon drawn. The room was unoccupied, but it was obvious that someone had lodged there. The bed wasn't made and the waste basket overflowed with empty beer cans. I also noticed what looked like drops of blood on the nightstand.

Though I feared for Karen's safety, I was equally concerned about the warning Jacobs gave me. I didn't know at the time, but the two baboons he'd seen were Rainey and Jackson Melbourne. While the silky-haired goons had earned an enviable reputation in their own right, lessons learned at the feet at their uncle, Zeek Wilcox, had taken them to places they never dreamed possible. Those enormous henchmen were like a couple of youngsters seeking the guidance and attention of a father figure. Under normal circumstances, two impeccably dressed young men like the Melbournes wouldn't have garnered a second look. Still, I wasn't of a mind to take them lightly. After all, these boys were the obedient lap dogs of a very dangerous man. Their very nature reeked of corruption and violence. They were capable of anything. Most importantly, they were standing right behind me!

Since the element of surprise was no longer an option, I decided to try a more audacious approach. So I spun around and pointed my gun directly at them. I would've expected such a daring maneuver to throw the average thug off his game, but the tempered assassins were a little too crafty for smoke and mirrors.

Jackson promptly disarmed me and scrambled my brain with a well-placed backhand! I went tumbling across the surface of the solid oak table in the corner.

Though it hardly seemed the time or place for reminiscing, I was besieged by an old memory as I hit the floor. I recalled the first match Awesome Anson English ever lost. He was defeated by a smaller opponent who descended upon him from the top rope. While attempting to catch the much lighter opponent, English lost his balance fell to the mat. I was certain a man my size could stagger a couple of lumbering stooges like the Melbournes if I moved fast enough.

Therefore, throwing caution to the wind, I sprang to my feet and charged the outlaws, convinced I could take them off their feet like a human clothesline. I was partly right. Jackson and Rainey did catch me, but they didn't fall down. Instead, the powerful gangsters lifted my body over their heads and hurled it across the room like a sack of potatoes. I landed between the bed and the wall.

Even in my semiconscious state, I recognized the need for a radical change in strategy.

On the other hand, the Melbournes were quite pleased with their performance and they didn't appear to need a break.

Appreciating that nothing can bring a formidable bruiser down more efficiently than his own arrogance, I prepared to play the trump card that terrified every criminal who'd ever heard of me.

Rainey strutted around the bed with a maniacal grin on his face. The conceited hulk was certain that I was putty in his hands. I just remained still and let him bait his own hook. When the chuckling idiot reached down, I suddenly exploded into his abdomen with my shoulder and retired his number with a searing right cross that sent him crashing through the bathroom door! He was done for the day.

Jackson wasn't about to challenge the legend of the killer knuckle sandwich without insurance. The policy he presented was in the form of a shiny switchblade knife. There were about nine feet between him and the sliding glass door to his left. In my present condition, I needed a lot of room to get around his cutter. That thing was huge.

I moved closer with my hands apart. The expression on the would-be slasher's face was intense, but I didn't let him intimidate me. When Jackson lunged forth, I leaped to one side and shoved him down on the bed as I ran out onto the terrace!

I darted across the redwood deck and looked over the edge. I could see people swimming in the pool, but the turquoise awning obstructed my view of the other guests. Thankfully, a police unit had just arrived. Although I considered jumping the waist-high rail and attempting a five-story swan dive, there was no way to determine whether or not the awning would break my fall. My only choice was to stand my ground and face the soulless foe head-on. As expected, he emerged through the sliding glass door ready to rumble.

Carefully calculating every move, Jackson stepped toward me, swinging the knife with unyielding conviction. I shuffled about the balcony, eluding the offensive as I waited for an opening.

With a well-timed kick to the rib cage, I brought the exhausted Neanderthal to his knees and endeavored to finish him off with a raging left hook! The knife fell at my feet as the basted bruiser hit the canvass. I thought the tide was turning my way, but when I reached down to retrieve his weapon, he took me off my feet with a sweeping kick.

Shellacking the redwood with my upper torso nearly left me breathless. Nevertheless, I maintained the presence of mind to raise my legs and thwart the charging mutilator's haphazard attempt to get his hands around my throat.

With all the force I had left, I pressed my feet against Jackson's chest and catapulted him off the balcony! I got up and made it to the edge in time to watch his enormous carcass strike the awning below. It looked like he was going to stay put until the clumsy slayer tried to stand up. That's when he lost his balance and went tumbling down into the breakfast buffet. Fortunately, a guest witnessed what was happening and warned the others to take cover. Though I was pleased to see that Jackson was still alive, it would be a long time before I could enjoy a plate of grits and eggs again.

With the Melbourne Brothers temporarily subdued and a couple of police officers on their way up, I presumed the worst was over. My powers of perception were in serious need of a tune up.

My missing revolver should've been the first indication that all wasn't well. When I went back inside, the peace had vanished from the spot where Jackson kicked it out of my hand. I ran across the room and began searching near the foot of the bed. It didn't occur to me that someone might have been lying in wait to pop me with my own gun.

I was about to overturn the mattress when a young blond woman stormed out of the closet with a baseball bat! Before I could say anything, the frightened slugger aimed for the bleachers with a line-drive across my injured shoulder. I was really getting tired of being hit from behind by desperate women.

I fell to the floor, clutching my aggravated wound, as I watched her run out into the hallway. Once she made it to the first floor, I knew she'd be gone for good. So I forced myself up and attempted to pursue the departing bat bandit, unaware that the officers I saw from the terrace had just stepped off the elevator. I made it around the corner just as the cops were taking her down.

"Let go of me, you pigs!" she shouted. "I didn't do anything. I want my lawyer!"

The brazen adolescent with the twenty-three year old temerity was on the floor ranting and screaming like a toddler. It was as though she didn't have an inkling why her universe was suddenly falling apart.

Considering the twists and turns this case had taken, it was possible that a precocious kid with little direction could've fallen in love with the son of Zeek Wilcox. On the other hand, she may have been the driving force that compelled him to assault Jodie Parker and abduct Karen Fuller. Either way, this young lady had a lot of explaining to do.

CHAPTER 25

I dropped by the hospital to let the doctors have a look at my aching shoulder. Although I could've done without the forty minute lecture on the responsibilities of a conscientious patient, I was glad to hear them say there was no permanent damage. They just gave me a shot and redressed the wound. Everything was going to be fine.

I wanted to feel the same way about Connie and Karen, but the forecast was looking gloomier by the minute. I'd encountered three people who knew where Wilcox had stashed the girls. Yet, they had every reason to keep their mouths shut. After all, the strongest case the State Attorney could put together wouldn't hold water if the star witnesses were nowhere to be found. For reasons beyond my comprehension, Brandi and the Melbourne Brothers were bound by a sense of loyalty that would take more than the dread of a prison sentence to overcome.

Even if his nephews could be persuaded to make things easier on themselves and blow the whistle on Uncle Zeek, I feared the change might be in vain. Time was not on our side.

Despite my disheartening outlook, I was encouraged by the concern and dedication of Sergeant Van Eason. In the wake of an explosion that threatened to annihilate his career, this compassionate man of honor had chosen to set aside his own concerns and move forward with the investigation.

It had been a long day for my old pal. He'd spent four grueling hours being pulled in all directions by a commission of vultures who wanted to pluck the stripes from his navy blue sleeves. No one would have blamed him for taking the rest of the day off and getting lost, but that wasn't Roy's way. He was determined to finish what he'd started. The most feasible means to that end involved a terrified young woman whose story sounded very familiar.

Her name was Brenda Elisha Anderson, but she preferred to be called Brandi. Beneath a skillfully crafted mask of rouge, lipstick and eye shadow, this vexing seventeen-year-old could've easily passed for twenty-five. Getting a handle on the tormented young player wasn't going to be easy. Outwardly, she exhibited the innocence of a wayward adolescent who'd do anything to procure the kindness and acceptance she didn't find at home. Yet, her rap sheet composed the portrait of an experienced scam artist who knew just how and where to get what she wanted. With a single twirl of that curly blond mane, the spirited temptress could send the life of an unsuspecting patsy into a tailspin. Although there were obvious chinks in her armor, when it came to the art of manipulation, this kid had skills and she wasn't afraid to put them to use.

Brandi didn't say a word as she watched Sergeant Van Eason and me enter the room and take our seats. She just glared straight ahead with those penetrating green eyes.

Van Eason laid a file on the table in front of her. "You're in a lot of trouble, Miss Anderson," he said. "We've already charged you with the assault on Mr. Masters. I suspect kidnapping will soon be added to the list."

"Kidnapping!" she gasped. "Who's been kidnapped?"

"Karen Fuller," Roy responded.

"She wasn't kidnapped," the uninformed suspect attempted to explain. "Chuck was just keeping her safe so this rent-a-cop here couldn't take her back to her abusive daddy."

"Is that what he told you?" I asked.

"Don't talk to me, creep!" she snapped. "You're the one who should be in jail."

"You've really got it in for Mr. Masters," Roy observed.

"He works for Karen's father," she said. "He was hired to bring the kid home so that animal can have her all to himself."

"Where did you get your information?" I asked.

"Chuck told me!" she declared as if lightning had carved the words into the side of a mountain. "He told me everything about you and that pervert."

"You seem to believe everything your boyfriend tells you," Roy deduced.

"He'd never lie to me," she asserted.

"Then why do you keep calling him Chuck?" the Sergeant asked.

"Because it's his name," she insisted.

Roy opened the file and showed the naïve suspect a mug shot of the man she knew as Chuck Wheeler. "His real name is Paul Wilcox," he told her. "He's a con man and a thief."

The impenetrable barrier that had shielded the heart of this daring young woman was beginning to crumble. The look of betrayal and disbelief was disturbing. Tears rolled down her cheeks as her lower lip trembled. "It's a trick," she muttered. "You're trying to set us up."

"It's no trick, Brandi," I assured her. "Wilcox has been lying to you all along. Karen's father couldn't have been abusing her."

"How can you be so sure?" she asked.

"Because he's dead," I said.

Roy placed another photo in front of her. "Do you know this girl?" he asked.

"Should I?" she responded.

"This is Connie Stewart," the sympathetic peace officer tenderly explained. "She's Paul's sister."

Brandi picked up the picture and peered at the somber-eyed teenager like a long lost friend. "So that's her," she whispered.

"He's mentioned her," I said.

"He said he saw her last year in a grocery store in Youngstown," Brandi explained.

"How could he have known that this girl was his sister?" Roy asked.

"Two years ago he went to visit his grandmother at the nursing home," she continued. "The old lady had a lot of photographs of Connie in her room. He kept a few of them. That girl's image is burned into his brain."

"Where did his grandmother get the pictures?" I asked.

"She told Chuck that Connie's aunt came by to visit her and left them," Brandi said.

Roy looked at me. "Maxine," he said.

"Chuck loves Grandma Rita," Brandi continued. "When he was young, his father wasn't around and his mother abused him. Rita was the only one who ever showed him love." Brandi thought for a moment. "I wonder how much of that story is true."

"It sounds about right," Roy commented.

"What do you mean?" she asked.

"The treatment he received from his mother explains the violence he exhibits toward women," Roy continued.

Brandi didn't seem surprised by Van Eason's assessment of her boyfriend. She just lowered her head and looked away.

"Has he ever hit you?" I asked.

"He gets frustrated," she said. "He doesn't mean to lose his temper."

"Even after all you've learned, you're still making excuses for him," the Sergeant said.

"In his own way, I believe Chuck loves me," she muttered as though she were trying to convince herself.

"If he loved you, he wouldn't use your face for a punching bag," I contended.

"There is something else you need to consider, Brandi," Van Eason added. "If you truly meant something to this man, he wouldn't have placed you in danger. He certainly wouldn't have left you holding the bag when the cops showed up. You don't owe him anything. Paul's dad has Karen Fuller and he's not going to give her the opportunity to finger them in court. So if you know anything that can help us find her, you need to speak up now."

Brandi clutched her forehead and sighed. "How did I get into this?" she lamented. "I just wanted the guy to love me. How could I have been so stupid?"

"You're not stupid, Brandi," I told her. "You just wanted something real. There's no crime in that."

"Before Mr. Masters came to my room at the Peddler's Lodge Inn, I overheard Chuck telling Rainey and Jackson not to let the girl leave the warehouse," she admitted.

"Do you know which warehouse he meant?" Roy asked.

"No," she replied. Brandi wiped her eyes and looked up at the ceiling. "I thought I was protecting her."

"Where are your parents, child?" the Sergeant inquired.

"I guess they're still in Daytona living their pure and faultless lives," she responded with a frown. "You can bet they aren't losing any sleep over me."

"That's where you're wrong," Roy said. "There has been an Amber Alert out on you for the past two years. They know they've made mistakes, but you've got to give a little, too."

"What do you know about any of this?" she asked.

"I know your father is on his way here," Van Eason informed her, as his voice cracked. "Your mother is very ill and she wants to see you. You've already seen what you can expect from the streets. It's time to go back to the people who really care about you. Take it from someone who knows, kid. You don't want to spend the rest of your life wishing you had one more day to set things straight." Roy stood up and looked at her. "I'm going to send an officer in here to tell you everything you need to know about the Wilcox Family and your mother's condition. She'll answer all your questions."

"What's going to happen to me?" Brandi asked.

"Well even though you thought you were protecting Karen, you were still an accessory to her abduction," he told her. "I don't know how the State Attorney will want to play it, but your cooperation will definitely be taken into consideration."

"And the assault," she inquired.

"I won't be pressing charges," I said, rising from my seat. "You've been given a chance to start over, Brandi. Don't take it for granted."

"Thanks," she said, placing her head on the table as she began sobbing.

Roy and I stepped out of the room and sent the officer in to speak with the shattered young woman. I could see the conversation with Brandi had taken a toll on my old friend.

"You all right, Sarge?" I asked.

"It has to work out, Pete," he said, as we headed down the corridor. "I can't stand the thought of another family living in the shadow of what should have been done."

"You've done all you can, Roy. It's up to Brandi now. She seems to be on the right track."

"I guess you're right. She did tell us what she heard Wilcox tell his cousins. I just wish I knew where we could find that warehouse."

When we reached the Sergeant's office, I remembered a story I'd read in the newspaper. "Let me see the file on the Melbourne Brothers," I requested.

"They found Lina Pembleton," he said. "She'd been worked over pretty good, but the doctors expect a full recovery."

I looked up and placed my hand to my chin. "Did anything else happen?" I asked.

Roy knew what I meant. "She wasn't violated," he assured me.

"I'm grateful for that."

"Jackson Melbourne will probably be in the hospital for a while. In the meantime, the State Attorney has enough evidence to keep him and his brother busy for the next thirty years."

"I should hope so."

"We also caught a break on your missing ninja," he said, displaying a photograph of Frankie Sullivan. "We got this from an ATM surveillance camera. The little nut case was using a stolen debit card. He's a slick one, but we'll get him."

"I have no doubt," I responded.

"What are you looking for, Gumshoe?" the frustrated Task Force Commander inquired.

"Roy, when I called the Fort Meyers Police Department, Captain Greg Perry told me the Melbourne Brothers had an interesting M.O. They would secure jobs under fictitious identities and spend several days casing the places they planned to rob."

"What does that have to do with Karen's abduction?"

"According to the police report, one of the items found in Rainey's car was an ID badge from the Creflo Muckerson Construction Company."

"So?"

"That company was building a warehouse for the Wexton Corporation until a local Native American tribe claimed the site was an ancient burial ground."

"What makes you think this warehouse is the one Wilcox mentioned?"

"Last month the tribe's attorney filed suit. The project is on hold and the structure is empty."

A look of anticipation swept over the Sergeant's face. "It would be the perfect place to hide a hostage!" he exclaimed.

"Exactly," I concurred.

"We'd better get out there."

After an exhausting uphill battle we'd finally stumbled across a lead that could blow the case wide open. Though Roy and I remained ever cautious of the dangers that lay ahead, we were eager to bring an end to the tormenting nightmare that had crippled the Stewart family for far too long. Now, the stage was set for the final act, and neither of us had any way of predicting how hard the curtain would fall.

CHAPTER 26

While I was certain the Wexton Corporation considered the enormous structure just off the Interstate to be an albatross that wouldn't die, discovering this achromatic assembly of concrete and steel sparked more hope than I'd embraced since the search for Connie Stewart began. Although located near the edge of the woods, it was adequately equipped to accommodate a family of fugitives who'd run out of options. With the aid of a stolen generator, several cooking appliances that were installed before construction was halted could've kept the Wilcox clan fed for at least another month. Considering the time of day, it would have been no surprise to find our resident robbers gathered around a table preparing to devour the spoils of conquest. Of course, Sergeant Van Eason and I intended to crash the party before Karen Fuller's invitation expired.

The warehouse wasn't far from completion. In fact, had the builders been allowed to proceed, this fifty-acre complex would've been bustling with activity. Instead, two bulldozers sat dormant, surrounded by stacks of cement bags. Discarded rivets and various scraps of metal debris were in the bed of a pickup truck that was parked a few yards from the front entrance. Selected portions of the property had been roped off so the archaeologists could go about their research. The secured garage door on the far side of the building was more than likely the area where Wilcox had chosen to station himself. It appeared to be the most strategic position in the warehouse. Moreover, I couldn't imagine a crafty fox like Zeek taking refuge without an avenue of escape. If the Corvette Connie and her biological father were driving when they pulled up to that convenience store in Vernon was still operational, I would've been willing to bet the farm that it was close by and ready to roll.

There wasn't a crack in the freshly laid asphalt when Roy parked the car behind a portable tool shed and radioed for backup. Waiting for more units would have been the prudent course of action, but the sun was setting and neither of us relished the idea of groping around in a dark death chamber. Furthermore, this was as close as anyone had gotten to Wilcox and we couldn't afford to wait any longer.

The intensity of the moment was all over Sergeant Van Eason's face. Regardless of the outcome, the lives of Karen and Connie were in his hands. That was enough to unnerve any man.

I'd hoped the special report that came over the radio when we left the station would make my good friend's burden a little lighter. The broadcast explained that a mistake had been made. The Native American burial ground that was alleged to be on this site was actually on a parcel of land several miles away. At least there was some solace in knowing we wouldn't be trampling the sacred soil of a people who'd already suffered more than their share of bigotry and demoralization.

Roy stepped out of the car and ran to the edge of the shed. After taking a second or two to look around, he beckoned for me to join him.

"We'll have to go in through the side entrance," he whispered, as I approached. "Keep your eyes open and measure every step. A psycho like Wilcox probably has this place booby trapped."

Staying low with our weapons drawn, we ran to the metal staircase leading up to a solid gray door. Fortunately, it wasn't locked. We cautiously entered the warehouse ready for anything.

"This is very disillusioning," I said.

"What is?" Roy asked.

"When I was a kid, my favorite television detective drove a convertible and had more girlfriends than he could handle. Now here I am lurking around in a creepy warehouse. It all feels like such a gyp."

"Take what you can get, cuz."

We found ourselves maneuvering down a narrow hallway with open doors on either side of us. Apparently, two of the entrances were going to be employee restrooms. A couple of sinks had been installed and there were copper pipes on the floor. The other doors were marked for storing chemicals and cleaning supplies.

We had to feel our way around until we reached the end of the tenebrous corridor. I was worried that the rest of the warehouse would be equally as difficult to make our way through, but once we stepped onto the concrete floor, I could see there were enough panes missing from upper level windows to provide the sunlight we needed. I should've been more concerned with what I couldn't see.

Rows of huge empty shelves seemed to go on forever. Stacks of pallets were all around us. A forklift with two missing wheels was parked near a pile of steel beams. Every instinct I had screamed trap. They were right.

Paul Wilcox and a compatriot named Barthelemy Krane stepped out into the open armed with a couple of .45 automatics.

Even though his criminal record wasn't extensive, the Sergeant and I were well acquainted with the escapades of Mr. Krane. In the nineties, the 300lb defensive end was the most talked about athlete in college sports. Yet, when assault allegations from women he'd dated began to sully his reputation and jeopardize future endorsements, the prideful icon snapped. Giving in to the fear of a life spent in poverty, Krane eventually attached himself to some of the most vicious crime bosses in town. For the right price, a lone shark or extortionist could reap the rewards of unleashing this raging storm upon the terrified and desperate. His massive build and propensity for aggression helped him achieve the respect of underworld figures around the state. I suppose it was only a matter of time before Zeek Wilcox got in touch with him.

"Well what do we have here?" Young Wilcox asked with a self-assured smirk. "It appears the stone-face bumpkin and his sidekick finally found us. It's a shame they won't be around to enjoy the praise of a grateful community. Why don't you gentlemen put those guns away? You won't need them anymore."

"Is Connie alright?" I inquired as we lowered our weapons.

"She's fine," Paul said. "The kid comes from quality stock. All those years of living a lie would've driven most girls crazy. Trying to keep up appearances among those suburban hypocrites had to be murder, but that's all in the past now. Connie's with her family and she's going to make us proud."

"How can anyone be proud of what you people do?" Van Eason asked. "You steal from the innocent and prey on the weak. How dare you talk about family pride! The only thing you should feel is shame."

I didn't know what my old friend had in mind, but ticking this punk off didn't seem like the most effective means to a peaceful end.

"Shut up, you keystone plowboy!" Paul demanded, slapping the uniformed officer to the floor. "You don't know a thing about my life. You hide behind that badge and gun, taking potshots at anyone who fails to live up to your standards."

I took a step toward my fallen colleague, but Krane was right on cue with his handgun pointed at my head.

"Stay where you are, Masters." The disaffected monster admonished.

"You guys are crazy," I said. "You've had a long run, but no one stays on top forever. Sooner or later, the man is going to shut you down. Give it up, kid."

"You should've been a lawyer, Masters," Wilcox said. "You make a very persuasive argument. But I wasn't born yesterday, big man. I wanted to give you the pleasure of watching me take out the fat chick. However, we are running out of time. I guess you'll just have to be satisfied with seeing your redneck friend get his first."

When Wilcox pointed his gun at Roy, I could tell by the gleam in his eye that the time for talking was over. I had to do something. Yet, I was trapped between a rock and a hard place. Even if I moved fast enough to take one of these bozos down, the other would surely kill Roy. Nothing short of an earthquake could buy me the time I needed. Ironically, I never expected it to come from someone who would've been more than happy to break out the champagne at my funeral.

Win, lose or draw, I'd decided to make my move and charge Wilcox. I tackled the young swindler to the floor and prepared to take one in the back. As expected, Krane took aim and pulled back the hammer.

That day would've gone down in history as my last stand if my huge would-be assassin hadn't been startled by what sounded like a dynamite blast! The diversion provided the opening Roy needed to spring to his feet and send the astounded cyclops crashing through a pile of wooded crates with a flying kick to the chest! I finished young Wilcox off with a chop to the back of the neck.

We'd taken care of the most immediate obstacles standing between the well-being of two teenage girls and the threat of imminent disaster. Nevertheless, our troubles were far from over. That fact was made abundantly clear when two masked intruders dressed in black came charging in!

The first man snatched off his mask and glared at me like an angry lion. There was no mistaking the hate in those eyes. It was Frankie "The Ninja" Sullivan. The psychotic weasel had finally caught up with me and he wasn't alone.

"I wanted the last face you saw in this life to be mine, Masters," the pompous thrasher said.

"Blowing the door off its hinges was a nice touch," I told him.

"Leaving a little fanfare for the press was the least I could do," he responded. "After all, I am going to kill you."

Roy pulled out his knight stick and began twirling it by the handle as he moved toward Sullivan's partner. Displaying no sign of apprehension, the masked bruiser assumed his fighting stance and prepared to strike.

Under ordinary circumstances, I would've assisted the tenacious Sergeant, but I was confident the fourth-degree black-belt was more than capable of handling his business. I, on the other hand, was about to engage a vengeful crazy man bent on ridding the planet of my odious presence. For some reason, things always seemed to turn out that way.

The martial arts nightmares wasted no time showcasing their murderous abilities. High sweeping kicks and deadly reverse punches were exhibited with flawless agility as these elusive phantoms in black encircled us.

Hoping to intimidate his much older opponent, Sullivan's partner bombarded Van Eason with a series of kicks and turns intended to bring the veteran law-enforcement officer to his knees. Nevertheless, undaunted by the masked slayer's offensive, the Sergeant evaded the lethal blows and waited for the perfect moment to thrust his knight stick into the young assassin's stomach before employing a spinning kick that plastered the wall with his descending carcass!

The action seemed to excite Sullivan. His demonstration of virtual destruction was equally impressive. The raging butcher even threw in a flying somersault for dramatic effect.

Like the instinctive flatfoot I called my friend, I also managed to elude my adversary's perilous advance by bobbing and weaving until the right opportunity presented itself. So I patiently waited for him to make the slightest misstep and proceeded to ring his chimes with my pulverizing right cross. That's when everything went to pot. The missed swing left me open to a slide blade kick that caught me in the rib cage. Sullivan then floored me with an old-fashioned shoulder-block.

Roy attempted to run to my aid, but his fallen opponent promptly cleared the cobwebs and attacked my would-be rescuer from behind. With his arm locked tightly around his victim's neck, the masked brawler endeavored to obstruct Van Eason's breathing.

Our situation would have appeared hopeless if I hadn't spotted a crowbar beneath the shelf a few inches from my head. I remembered the injury Sullivan sustained the last time we faced off. I had no desire to cripple the young viper, but time was running out and bringing Zeek Wilcox down would require all the energy I had left. So with tempered exertion, I picked up the crowbar and popped the Ninja on the side of his injured knee.

In the blink of an eye, the tables had turned. Sullivan fell to the floor clutching his throbbing joint. The Ninja's outcry distracted his crony enough to make him loosen the grip he had around the Sergeant's neck. Without warning, Van Eason planted an elbow into the masked man's sternum and put him away with a searing backhand!

I ran over to Roy. "Are you okay, slugger?" I asked him.

"I'm fine," he responded. "We'd better get the cuffs on Krane and the kid."

"What about the other two?"

"Backup is on the way. Let's gather up their guns and find the girls...Oh and one more thing, Pete."

"Yeah."

"This is a man who trained his children to be savage criminals. Don't take him for granted."

"Understood."

After securing the area, the Sergeant and I set out to find Zeek Wilcox. We decided to split up in case there were more gorillas lurking around. Roy headed down the middle aisle while I stayed near the wall to his right.

With the time Paul and Barthelemy Krane had bought him, I didn't expect Zeek to be hanging around when we reached the other end of the warehouse. However, I wasn't aware that he was being detained by something too precious to leave behind.

At the moment he was preparing to make his escape, Connie was beginning to understand the true nature of the father she thought she knew. The conversation was a bit vague, but with every step I could hear this master manipulator reveal the man he was inside.

Karen was trembling in a chair bound and gagged. Everything was in place. There was only one item of business that needed to be completed.

"It's time, kid," Wilcox said, handing Connie his .380 semiautomatic handgun.

"Time for what?" the bewildered teen inquired.

"Are you kidding me? People must've heard that explosion for miles. We've got to hit the road!"

"Aren't you going to wait for Paul?"

"We don't have time. Besides, your brother has been in tighter spots than this. He'll make it out. Now take that rod and uphold your obligation to this family."

Connie didn't have to ask what he meant. The look in his eyes said it all.

"I can't," she said. "Karen is my closest friend. She stood by me when no one else cared. How can you ask me to do this?"

The expression of the demented father's face became more intense. "Your loyalty should be to your family!" he insisted. "Now put a bullet in this girl's noggin and let's get out of here."

Wilcox ran over to start the car and open the automatic garage door. In those few seconds, the self-centered fagin became painfully aware of the differences between Connie and his other children. This child had a conscience. She wasn't about to betray the love of a trusted friend. She just stood there crying as her nervous hands lowered the gun.

"I don't believe you!" Wilcox exclaimed, approaching the girls. "Maybe you're just not cut out to be one of us. Now give me that piece."

"No!" she undauntedly refused.

"What?"

"I'm not going to let you kill her. You're always talking about family honor, but it's all one-sided. You don't have the slightest qualm about leaving Paul behind for the cops. You didn't bat an eye when you found out about Jackson and Rainey. You're the one who needs to learn something about loyalty."

The offended fugitive slapped his daughter to the floor! "Just who do you think you're talking to, little girl?" he asked. "I've given you everything. You didn't even know what living was until you found me. If you want to go back to your suburban nine-to-five existence, be my guest. But you'd better get one thing straight. I didn't make it this far by being stupid. This girl can identify me and other members of the family. She needs to be taken out."

Wilcox reached down and picked up the gun that was lying beside his daughter's foot.

All the clarity Connie had been seeking came flooding through her mind. She'd placed everyone she loved in danger. The repentant runaway didn't know whether or not there was still time to right the wrongs she'd committed, but she wasn't going to let this psycho kill her best friend. So when Wilcox aimed the gun at Karen, Connie put it all on the line and charged him!

By this time, I'd reached a row of industrial washers and taken cover. After all the pavement pounding and near fatal assaults, I was finally a few paces away from the elusive villain who'd exacted so much misery upon the Sunshine State. In his blue jeans and faded denim jacket, the bearded hustler with the silky ponytail didn't look so intimidating. Of course, it would've been difficult for anyone to embody the attributes of a fearless gangster while struggling to keep a gun away from a frightened sixteen-year-old girl.

"Hold it right there, Wilcox!" I admonished.

For a half-second that seemed to go on forever, Wilcox and Connie stopped and looked in my direction. During the past few weeks, I'd learned a lot about this selfish creep, but his next move turned out to be an act of cowardice that even surprised me. The besieged bandit spun Connie around and placed the gun to her head.

"Don't get any crazy ideas, pig!" he shouted. "I'm sure you don't want this kid's life on your conscience."

Shielded behind the slender frame of his beguiled teenage daughter, Wilcox cautiously shuffled backward until the two of them reached the open driver's side door of his idling Corvette.

"No!" Connie screamed, struggling to break free from the man she thought she knew.

"Are you crazy?" Wilcox shouted, endeavoring to maintain control. "You can't stay here. They'll put you in jail."

Connie fell to the floor and attempted to crawl away. Wilcox reached down to pick her up just before a blast from the darkness pierced the front fender! Realizing he had no choice but to leave his child, the savvy gangster raised his firearm and began shooting at random, as he leaped into the front seat.

When Wilcox sped away, I wanted to make sure the person who fired the last shot at the fleeing felon was on my side. So I laid low and waited for him to step out into the open. Thankfully, the uniformed gunman looked very familiar.

"Roy!" I cried out.

"Come out, Pete," the Sergeant responded.

We ran to the edge of the sally port and fired at the speeding vehicle, but our final assault was to no avail. Suddenly, the sounds of police sirens filled the air as backup units began to descend upon the scene.

"You help Connie up and I'll untie Karen," Roy instructed.

I walked over and gently took the young women's hand. The tears that flowed from her betrayed brown eyes spoke volumes. This kid had been down a long, dark road and I could see how much she regretted every step of the way.

"I thought he loved me," she said, rising to her feet. "He said he was going to pull one more job and use the money to buy a place in Mexico for all his children. Was everything he told me a lie?"

"I'm afraid so, honey," I told her. "Zeek Wilcox is a thief and a con man who only loves himself."

"He was going to make me kill Karen. It didn't matter how good she'd been to me. He just wanted to make sure she couldn't point the finger at him. All that talk about family was worthless garbage."

"He's only loyal to himself. But I know someone who has loved you from the very beginning."

"How could he still want me back after all I've done?"

"Because Michael is a real father."

When Roy freed Karen, the teary-eyed young woman walked over to the friend she loved like a sister.

"Karen, I'm so sorry," Connie said, as she wondered what was going through her girlfriend's mind. "I believed the rubbish Paul and Zeek drilled into my brain. I thought it was the way I was born to live. I know how pathetic it sounds, but I needed to feel like I belonged to someone. Can you ever forgive me?"

Karen's eyes were blackened and her cheeks were bruised. Tears streaked down her face as she reached out to take Connie's hands. "You are my sister," she said. "Nothing will ever change that."

Though Roy and I were impressed by the strength of the bond that cemented these girls, I could see the trepidation on the Sergeant's face.

"What is it, Roy?" I asked.

"Wilcox isn't used to having his plans run amok," he explained. "There's no telling what kind of havoc he's capable of wreaking now. And we don't have a clue where he might have headed."

"I know," Karen said.

"Where?" I inquired.

"I heard him tell his son that every link to them had to be eliminated," she told us. "He said they couldn't leave town until my mother and Connie's father were history…Please don't let him hurt our parents!"

"Don't worry, Kiddo," I said. "We're going to do everything we can."

"He took the Interstate," Roy lamented. "It'll take a miracle to catch him now."

"Not if I know my shortcuts," I said. "We should get to Karen's house in time to greet Big Daddy with a pair of handcuffs."

"Then let's go," the Sergeant responded.

Zeek Wilcox had pulled more than his share of sleazy stunts in the past, but this time he was determined to commit murder. There wasn't a moment to lose. A depraved killer was on his way to pay Mollie Fuller a surprise visit, and we had to get there before he became the last guest she would ever entertain.

CHAPTER 27

My estimated time of arrival didn't exactly hit the bull's eye. By the time Zeek Wilcox broke into Mollie's house and began looking around, the nearest patrol unit was still several blocks away.

Sergeant Van Eason parked his vehicle in a vacant lot at the corner. We took different routes and headed for the Fuller residence. It was almost dark, so we weren't worried about attracting too much attention. An officer had placed a call warning Mollie to vacate the premises. I thought that was the reason why her car wasn't in the driveway, but when I made it to the house across the street, the glare of approaching headlights proved me wrong.

I took cover behind a couple of garbage cans and waited to see who was driving. To my dismay, it was Mollie. She retrieved three bags of groceries from the back seat and proceeded toward the house. I was about to call out to her when I noticed Zeek Wilcox peering out the kitchen window. Startling a nut like him could have spelled disaster. So I waited until Mollie was inside and scurried across the street.

I could hear the two of them struggling as I reached the welcome mat. The back door was cracked open enough for me to observe the monster in action. Frozen food was scattered about the top of the counter and the refrigerator door was wide open. Mollie's ruby red pumps had made huge black marks across the surface of her recently waxed floor. If I'd gotten there a minute earlier, I could've caught Wilcox by surprise, but that opportunity had passed. All I could do was watch helplessly as he clung tightly to his female hostage and kept that huge butcher knife to her throat.

"Not a word, sister!" Wilcox admonished. "You're a hot old broad. I'd hate to mangle that gorgeous face of yours."

"What do you want?" the terrified victim asked.

"Shut up! I'll ask the questions. Where's Michael Stewart?"

"He said he was going to the police station."

"I guess I'll have to find a way into that den of pigs and take him out right under their noses. Ah well...It wouldn't be the first time."

Mollie wasn't sure where Michael was, but she certainly wasn't going to help this animal ambush her old friend. "Who are you?" she asked.

"I'm the guy who's going to make sure you and your daughter are united forever," he responded.

Tears flowed down the frightened mother's cheeks. "Zeek Wilcox," she muttered. "What have you done with my little girl?"

"Oh she's still alive. But I wouldn't plan the family barbecue just yet. As soon as I shake the cops, I'm coming back to take care of her, too."

"What kind of man are you? You're talking about killing a teenage girl as if it was just another day at the office. You've trained your own children to be con artists and thieves. You're nothing but an evil monster. And someday, you'll get what you deserve."

Wilcox grabbed a handful of his hostage's hair and pulled her head back. "Now why don't we cut out all this chitchat and start walking?" he said.

Mollie couldn't have chosen a more volatile moment to let Wilcox know what she thought of him. He wasn't used to being challenged and I had no way of predicting how he'd react once he determined I was only a few feet away. I thought about trying to pick him off, but the rattled intruder was too close to his captive.

"Where are we going?" Mollie asked.

"To the bedroom, hot stuff," he responded. "But don't you worry that pretty little head about anything. I'm not going to hurt you. I promise there won't be any nightmarish recollections to torture you. After all, it's hard to be plagued by bad memories when you're dead."

With the knife held closely to the woman's throat, Wilcox accompanied her into the living room where they turned right and proceeded down the dimly lit hallway leading to her bedroom.

There was no way I could have made it across that kitchen floor without attracting attention, so I crept around the side of the house, looking for another way inside.

The first window I came to gave me a perfect view into the house. I was about to break in when I heard the sounds of Mollie and Wilcox struggling. Letting the assailant catch me entering the room would've left me vulnerable. So I took cover behind an elm tree and waited.

It was obvious that Wilcox had spent a considerable amount of time snooping through his intended victim's belongings. Empty drawers that had been snatched from the dressers mingled among the lady's scattered unmentionables. The sliding wooden doors to her closet were also cracked open. There was no doubt he'd enjoyed invading Mollie's privacy. Yet, the condition of the room wasn't the most disturbing element of this cerebral odyssey.

Wilcox had left a belt and a roll of duct tape on Mollie's satin pillow. His eyes danced as he observed her dumbfounded reaction.

"Take off your coat," he told her.

The woman complied with her encroacher's instructions and covered her upper torso with the blazer. "What are you going to do?" she inquired.

"Don't worry. I promise you'll have a good time."

I gleaned from Mollie's expression that she had something in mind. Accustomed to thinking on her feet, she suddenly threw the garment over the deviant's head and decked him with all the strength she could muster!

Unfortunately, the impromptu offensive barely staggered the street-hardened brawler. He had both arms securely around her waist before she could make it out of the room.

Unwilling to risk another escape attempt, Wilcox promptly tied Mollie's hands to the headboard with the belt and placed a strip of tape over her mouth.

"That ought to teach you some manners," the conceited fagin boasted, as he began severing the buttons from her blouse with the knife. "You're a feisty chick. The two of us are going to have a real good time. You've just got to relax."

It was out of character for Wilcox to lose focus over a pretty face. He'd swindled some of the most attractive women in the state. Making some rich widow believe the moon and stars were put in place to illuminate their beauty was all part of doing business. Yet, this time the old fox was dazzled and intrigued. In fact, it never occurred to him that someone might have been watching through the parted curtains on the other end of the room.

Though I was bewildered, it appeared the odds were finally in my favor. The man who'd gotten away with so much for so long was now cornered and I had a clear shot. So I pulled back the hammer and took aim. I was sure that nothing would stand in the way of bringing Zeek Wilcox to justice. Sadly, like so many times before, I was wrong.

I didn't know Michael Stewart had been biding his time in the closet, waiting for Wilcox to let his guard down. Without warning, Mollie's valiant companion stormed across the bedroom floor and tackled the surprised intruder like a raging bull! The two of them shuffled around the room, bouncing off walls as they battled for control of the knife.

Michael didn't stand a chance against a skilled fighter like Wilcox. I had to get in there.

The only object on the ground that looked capable of shattering the window was a ceramic frog. So I picked up the huge green eyesore and hurled it through the glass. I was amazed at how quickly Wilcox was able to stash Michael back into the closet and produce his semiautomatic handgun before I could make my way in. He got off three rounds and headed for the living room where Sergeant Van Eason was waiting in the darkest section of the room with his weapon drawn.

"It's the end of the line, Wilcox," the Sergeant said. "Give it up before anyone else gets hurt."

This confident gunman had beaten the odds in more than a few shootouts. His speed and accuracy with a firearm were nothing less than phenomenal. However, this time, he wasn't fast enough.

Van Eason dropped him with a single round that sent him crashing into the screen of the fifty-four inch High-Definition television set in the corner!

Even the impressive skills of a surprisingly superior opponent were not enough to extinguish the fire in this inherent survivor. Despite the glass and other debris, Wilcox attempted to slither across the bloodstained carpet and retrieve his gun. He'd almost reached the weapon when he felt the weight of a large foot pressing down on his wrist. The defeated villain looked up and saw the barrel of my revolver pointed down at his head.

"Bad idea, Daddy Dearest," I said.

Van Eason approached with a set of handcuffs and bound the suspect's hands behind his back.

"I'm bleeding here!" Wilcox shouted. "I need a doctor."

At that moment, we could hear the screams of approaching sirens.

"Help is on the way," the Sergeant said. "We're not like you. We take no pleasure in the suffering of others."

Before we could bring Wilcox to his feet, there was a knock at the door. Two of Roy's patrolmen had just arrived. "Sarge!" One of them called out.

"It's all clear, boys," their commanding officer responded. "Come on in."

Like my old friend, I thought the worst was over, until the officers entered the residence. That's when Connie and Karen appeared in the doorway.

"I told you girls to stay in the car," Roy chided.

"We want to see our parents," Connie insisted. "Are they alright?"

"This way," Karen said, as the two of them headed for the bedroom.

"Come back here!" Van Eason demanded.

"I'll go, Roy," I said. "You take care of Wilcox."

I pursued the girls to Mollie's room. Karen ran to her mother and endeavored to set her free while Connie approached the closet where Michael was standing. Only his head was visible. The rest of his body was concealed behind the partially closed doors. Connie had anticipated an embrace, but the expression on her adoptive father's face gave cause for wonder. Why didn't he come running with open arms? Had months of sadness and worry melted into resentment? At any rate, Connie wasn't going to let personal anxiety ruin this long awaited reunion. The best she could do was just be prepared for anything.

"Daddy," the nervous prodigal daughter spoke. "I'm back."

"You don't know how many times I've prayed for this moment, honey," Michael told her.

"I know I did some terrible things before I left and I'm so sorry. I got caught in a storm of lies and foolishness."

"That's all behind you now, kid," Michael said with labored breath.

"Are you alright?" Connie asked.

"I'm fine, but I want you to listen to me. In the days to come, you're going to hear things about your mother and Maxine that won't be easy to accept. I just hope you'll be understanding and remember that love makes us act crazy at times."

"What are you talking about, Daddy?"

"You'll see. I also want you to get in touch with Horace Kemper. He handles my finances. There is more than enough money for you to get through college and make a good life for yourself. I know you've made mistakes, but you don't have to keep beating yourself up. None of us are perfect. You've been a real treasure to me, angel. No matter what anyone says, you are and will always be my daughter."

Connie's heart was breaking. Moved by her father's sentiments, she parted the doors and reached out to touch him. That's when she discovered what he'd been hiding. Michael's shirt was soaked with blood and the life was seeping from his body.

"Daddy!" the girl cried. "What happened to you?"

Even in his anguish, the last touch from this precious child's hand made him smile. "Don't worry, baby," he said. "Everything is going to be alright. I love you."

Suddenly the smile vanished from Michael's face as he fell forward and landed at his daughter's feet with the butcher knife protruding from his side!

"No!" Connie screamed.

I approached him and check for a pulse, but it was too late. Michael was dead. "I'm sorry, Connie," I said.

I stepped back as Mollie and Karen attempted to comfort the inconsolable teen. They knelt beside her and tried to ease her pain, but there was nothing anyone could do. An invaluable gem in the hearts of these three women was gone and nothing would ever fill that void.

Tears flowed like a river for the man who'd sacrificed so much in the name of love. In my efforts to keep him strong, I'd given rise to the promise of a better tomorrow. I was certain that the warmth and disposition of this extraordinary individual would always overcome the darkness.

Though my intentions were pure, I had to wonder whether or not there was an element to this equation that was beyond my understanding. Could there have been a more profound meaning to the tragedies Michael Stewart endured? Was there something we all had to learn that would take a lifetime to reveal itself? I guess the answers to those questions would have to remain with the source of greater wisdom than I could ever hope to possess.

Would you like to see your manuscript become a book?

If you are interested in becoming a PublishAmerica author, please submit your manuscript for possible publication to us at:

acquisitions@publishamerica.com

You may also mail in your manuscript to:

**PublishAmerica
PO Box 151
Frederick, MD 21705**

www.publishamerica.com

CPSIA information can be obtained at www.ICGtesting.com
Printed in the USA
LVOW040027170512

282063LV00002B/48/P